DRAGON BREATH
ZHANLUE

(STRATEGY)

DRAGON BREATH
ZHANLUE

(STRATEGY)

China's Quest to Rule the World

BY

JACK D. WAGGONER

ARPress
45 Dan Road Suite 5
Canton MA 02021
Hotline: 1(888) 821-0229
Fax: 1(508) 545-7580

Ordering Information:

Quantity sales. Special discounts are available on quantity purchases by corporations, associations, and others. For details, contact the publisher at the address above.

Printed in the United States of America.

ISBN-13:   Paperback   979-8-89356-410-5
                  eBook   979-8-89356-409-9

Library of Congress Control Number: 2024904451

Other books by Jack D. Waggoner

Birdnest
Flight to Puska
Rainbow Zhanlue (Strategy)
The Voyages Under Arcturus*
Killing ISIS*
God's Parallel Planets

*not yet published

Further Data

Author note: The reader can follow the process that started in 1998 by reading :

The Rainbow Zhanlue (Strategy)

Library of Congress No. 2011961184

ISBN Hardcover 978-1-4653-0837-5

ISBN Softcover 978-1-4653-0836-8

ISBN EBOOK 978-1-4653-0838-2

when you are godless
and evil
nothing
is outside your reach.

CHAPTER
1

The unmarked all-white Gulf-stream G650, with twin Rolls-Royce Pearl 700 turbofan engines, made a hot landing on the restricted airstrip that was located just outside the city of Baoding on the Chang Chia Tun military complex. Braking hard, the pilot overshot the last exit ramp, which necessitated a U-turn at the end of the runway. Once completed, he accelerated hard back up the strip to a taxi ramp that led to a large warehouse. The building was isolated from the rest of the military base by an intricate set of fences and barricades that were manned by special forces troops of the People's Liberation Army (PLA).

The structure was fully camouflaged with rooftop foliage and ground plants that when combined with an earth-tone paint scheme, made the building blend into the rolling hills and tree covered countryside. The entire area, within three kilometers of the site, was also manned by PLA Special Forces that kept prying eyes at bay.

As the jet pulled up to the building, massive doors opened automatically and the plane nosed into the hangar. The pilot nursed the ship toward a suspended light bar that made a soft clicking sound as the center support member of the windshield made a contact, at which point the pilot powered down the two big engines, set the brake, and commenced shutting down the flight systems.

Before the aircraft door could be cracked, the passengers experienced a sinking sensation as the floor of the hangar dropped down into total darkness. Finally lights from below materialized, and the elevator that the plane was riding nestled gently into a beautiful sunlit courtyard.

The passengers were greeted with a sight that only a handful of their countrymen would ever see. No palace entrance, anywhere, was more opulent. A red carpet stretched from the plane's door across a courtyard of magnificent green and white marble to a flight of eight steps that led to a sparkling golden glass ingress. On each of the wide marble steps, framing the entrance were highly decorated Chinese ceramic pots (each a breathtaking original from past dynasties) featuring gold inlays and ancient scenes, all from the Yuan Dynasty (1271-1368). The pots were filled with exotic tropical plants, and between each pot was a life-size earthen clay statue that had been taken from the Rent Courtyard Collection.

The president had put the life-size Rent Courtyard figures here, at the entrance to his personal command bunker, to remind himself and his comrades of their past. He never failed to stop and admire the work of his friend, the contemporary artist Cal Guo-Qiang, who had completed the collection in 1965. During China's Great Proletarian Cultural Revolution, the Rent Courtyard Collection was acclaimed a model sculpture in support of the revolution. The sculptures portrayed starving peasants, standing in a sinister landlord's sterile courtyard, struggling to pay the portion of grain demanded from them as rent.

The President stood next to a sculpture of a pathetic and downtrodden mother carrying her emaciated baby, both dressed in rags. He could see the pain and hurt in her eyes. It never failed to renew his sense of how far the revolution had come and how much he and his fellow countrymen owed to Mao and his nearly divine leadership. Whenever he looked at these pitiful clay figures, he rededicated his mind and body to eliminating such images from the Chinese landscape forever. There were no badges to show or guards to check the new arrivals. Each person in the president's party had a small computer chip implanted in their left earlobe. The scanning computer immediately notified everyone within the bunker that the President and his personal staff were in the facility. The computer system would track the president's movements until he departed from the underground complex.

The security team that oversaw the operation was led by a senior staff deputy that had been with the president since his rise from army grand general to Communist Party leader and then in 1997, to the station of supreme president.

Inside the golden glass doors, a vast three-story entry hall greeted the visitor. It was, in reality, a small museum with artwork from the greatest Chinese masters. Every dynasty was represented in the vases and the tapestries on the walls alongside contemporary and ancient paintings. It was a dazzling display of Chinese art and culture. The president never failed to take a few minutes upon arrival to stop and scrutinize different items, marveling at the artifacts that his ancestors had created. Today his attention was captured by a jade carving depicting sixteen prancing horses. The piece was about sixty centimeters long, thirty high and ten wide. Each of the steeds was in a different running, almost flying, position that made the entire piece seem alive and in motion. It reminded him of the Flying Horse of Kansu, the original of which was setting on his desk at his Beijing office.

Manes and tails flying, the piece was fashioned from white-green streaked jade that made it seem almost ghostlike. It had been carved from one solid chunk of jade and the detail was astonishing. You could almost see the wild stare of a young stallion as his pale-green eyes flashed. The sculpture was cold and hard yet somehow soft to the touch, and the president found himself stroking the back of the leading steed, wondering about the artist who created this incredible masterpiece.

It was almost as if he traveled back in time to the magical age of art that the Chinese brought to the world while the Europeans were still struggling through the dark ages. It was truly amazing, and as his thoughts of the past collided with the present, he remembered that this was to be a very important day. Returning to reality and looking around, he saw that his staff were all silently waiting for him to finish his passage back in time so they could continue theirs. Everyone knew this was going to be a special day. They were not sure about the details, but they could tell and sense that something big was in the works. The president smiled at each person as he continued to rub the nose of the lead horse.

In a low tone he said, "Thank you all for your service to the people." He continued in a nearly inaudible voice that made each listener strain to hear, "We are the glue that holds this wonderful country of ours together, and we all must continue *yi ren wei ben* (putting the people first). Go do your work for the people and remember this day. The world will change and you and I will be directing that change. It is the hardest work we shall ever do, but we each have a special strength derived from our ancestors." He took one last look at the sculpture in front of him, and the motion of the running stallions was like a cascading waterfall; motion that when started could not be stopped, and he was excited about the prospects of implementing his Dragon Breath Zhanlue.

President Yanlin Hu was proud to be Chinese and to invoke the memory of his ancestors, talking to them and asking for their advice, but those times were over. The plan was complete and ready to be put into action, a strategy that he was confident would change the world, not today or next year, but within ten years the world would start to change, and he would be the master pulling the strings. It was so simple but required great patience, and he was more than ready to get on with the project. His fingers lingered on the cold smooth jade that seemed to impart energy into his very fingertips. He could feel a tingle up his arm, and he looked down at the piece and wondered again who had created this incredible work of art. Who had labored to find the stone and then carve and polish it for decades to create this masterpiece? If his ancestors could labor over one piece of art for so long, he could wait for his Zhanlue and the resulting plan to come to fruition. Yes, he could wait. His finger slid off the lead stallion's nose and he turned to start the journey that would change the world.

At the far side of the entry hall were two elevators, one marked "up" and the other "down". The president moved across the marble floor with a renewed purpose. As he neared the down elevator the door opened automatically and the leader of the People's Republic and his loyal aide entered while the rest of the staff went to their various offices on the upper floors. The elevator dropped down to level 16, which when he was in the bunker complex served as his private quarters and office.

As the door opened, the president stepped out to be greeted by his old friend and security chief, Jet How Chung.

"Jet, it's good to see you," the president said as he put his arm around his old friend's shoulder and guided him toward the presidential offices.

"It is good to see you as well, Comrade President, and I am looking forward to the unveiling of your new Zhanlue."

"Yes, I am excited as well. It will be good to bring this matter to a conclusion. Do I assume that I have your undivided support?"

Jet How gave his mentor a smile and replied, "Of course," and then continued, "my support was never in question. Actually, I have been thinking about nothing else since you outlined the plan last month. I am looking forward to the challenge but have been wondering if you expect any resistance from the conservative members of the council?"

The president walked around the ornately carved wooden desk, sat down, put his feet up on one corner of the polished wood and replied, "No, I think not. In the long run they all know that we have to take this bold step in order to achieve our long-range goals. There are only two avenues open, all-out war or our Zhanlue and yes, I think the council will embrace our plan. Jet, this is going to be an incredibly difficult task, and it will require a great deal of money, but in the final analysis I don't think we have any choice." Smiling he added, "How much better is it to be the Trojan Horse than to risk an all-out nuclear war?"

Jet How nodded agreement as the president continued, "When it is done, we will truly be the dominant force in the world and the other nations will bow to our will once they see that America is under our control."

"You are right, of course, Comrade President, but what if the plan is leaked or compromised in some way that we cannot foresee or control? That would put us in a very bad light and might even give the Americans more power."

"Jet, I'm not worried about a leak. After all we are only talking about the five of us and I cannot envision any of the group making a slip or being disloyal. Remember two of them are the Old Guard. They have not forgotten when Mao chased Chiang Kai-shek out of China and they followed. They will be loyal. I feel it in my bones."

Jet How took off his glasses and looked directly into the president's black eyes and said, "Comrade, it certainly is a brilliant Zhanlue, and I cannot wait to get started."

Author Note:

In November of 1998 when William Jefferson Clinton was president of the United States of America the Chinese launched their Rainbow Zhanlue (Strategy) which was a long-range plan to transfer the wealth of America to China, i.e. "capture the pot of gold at the end of the rainbow." Nothing more, nothing less. A straight forward maneuver that would see China become the second wealthiest nation on the planet by the election cycle of 2016. Clinton, Bush and Obama were willing participants in that they did nothing, absolutely nothing to stop the bleeding, in fact they (Obama/Biden) were eager to give the farm away and in the process family members became super rich, at the expense of the great unwashed American public that the elites hold in such contempt. Hillary meant it when she called her fellow Americans a "BASKET OF DEPLORABLES."

In 1998 you could count the number of millionaires in China using your fingers and toes, but by 2018 that number would grow to 4.4 million as China overtook the USA in rankings of the world's richest people. At the Meifan Yacht Club, outside Beijing, you will not be considered for membership unless your yacht is longer than 100 meters. (300 feet)

In the seventeen years since President Hu unleashed The Rainbow Zhanlue (Strategy) on America the Chinese economy not only flourished but blossomed on a truly grand scale and is poised to surpass the U.S. economy early in the third decade of the twenty-first century. It did not happen by accident. It happened because the leaders of China decided that was their long-range goal and worked their plan.

CHAPTER

2

Thursday, June 25, 2015, had been hot and humid in the teaming Chinese metropolis of Beijing and despite the government's best efforts the air pollution was almost unbearable.[*]

The President of China had been glad to exchange Beijing's smog for the views that greeted him from his opulent underground bunker complex. The garden view, from his office, featured weathered pine trees and blooming dogwoods, combined with all manner of lush native plants that framed a stone bridge from the Tang Dynasty (618-906). The bridge spanned a splashing stream that exited a pool of sparkling blue water.

An incredible waterfall splashed and tumbled down from twenty-five meters above the pond, providing a cooling mist that blanketed the garden complex. The President and his guests could wander about the garden while a computer-controlled lighting system replicated the sun's rise and set. In fact, when one looked up, fluffy white clouds seemed to cross the sky, exactly like those at Caesar's Palace in Las Vegas.

Seated on a stone bench the Premier of China surveyed his underground kingdom and smiled the smile of the world's largest Cheshire Cat as he reveled in the success of his brilliant Rainbow Zhanlue. It was on this very spot that he had conceived the Zhanlue

* (The 54-coal fired electrical generating plants in China represent roughly 1,000 gigawatts of existing COAL capacity and there are approved plans to build another 121 gigawatts capacity, which is more than is being built in the rest of the world combined.)

(strategy) back in 1998 and seventeen years later the results were even more dramatic than he could have ever hoped. Some of his fellow council members, those that helped him implement the strategy, were no longer walking the planet, like General Fan Chang Long and Minister Yide Du, but fortunately Jet How Chung, Lin Wong and Admiral Cheng Wanquan were still in good shape and he was looking forward to the next few days of comradeship with his loyal supporters.

He had worked hard, he had beaten the odds and won the biggest gamble of his life. It had all paid off, in spades, as his professional gaming friends like to say.

Coming inside from their garden stroll, President Hu seated himself behind his Ming Dynasty desk and beckoned Jet to be seated in one of the elegant side chairs, which were from the Sui Dynasty (581-618). President Hu looked at his comrade, a deep look that Jet had come to expect. "Are you well my friend?" he asked.

"Yes, yes I'm certainly getting old, but I am well and my mental facilities seem to be unimpaired. Wish I could say the same for my wife, but the doctors think she is experiencing the first phases of Alzheimer's and so far there is no cure, so we just take it day by day. I can tell you with no hesitation, no hesitation whatsoever, that I feel more alive today than I have since we started the Rainbow Zhanlue in 1998. Those were special times comrade President and looking back on the events of the last, what seventeen years, we did one great job. Maybe the most impressive job any group of humans has ever done, don't you agree?"

"Yes, Jet, looking back I too marvel at what we were able to accomplish. Just think in 1998 we were barely in the top ten of exporting nations and today we are number one. The World Trade Organization help greatly but our Zhanlue to buy up America's wealth, on the backs of our workers, was brilliant, simply brilliant."

The President's eyes flashed, and he continued, "We muscled right over America and the Europeans and we did it with their blessing and complicity. No one challenged our theft of their intellectual properties, no one challenged our students-agents flooding their best colleges and universities. No one even challenged us when we took over control of the Panama Canal and no one even whimpered when we gave that little fat bug in Pyongyang the means to develop nuclear capability. That has kept the West occupied for the last forty years while we built our offshore islands and made inroads in every country on the face of the planet and in the process created 4.4 millionaires. Honestly, Jet if you had told me in 1998 that we would be where we are today, I would have thought you had been drinking hard liquor. I still pinch myself sometimes and yet it's true, all true and our new Zhanlue will make an even a bigger impact on the world and its peoples."

A thoughtful ear-splitting-smiling pause followed the president's pronouncements and finally Jet broke the silence by asking, "Comrade President, is it possible that you and I might be the only participants in this new Zhanlue?" "Jet, I don't doubt that we could handle the challenge but there are going to be lots of areas to cover and so I have decided to go with the established Group of Five. The three joining us in our discussions later today and into tomorrow will be Comrade Wong, Comrade Keshi and of course Admiral Wanguan." Jet looked over his glasses and nodding his head said, "Yes, those are good choices. Each has his expertise and each is trustworthy to the death. Good choices Comrade, I look forward to working with them."

"Jet, you may have wondered why the Vice President or any of his supporters are not included, and that is because I am still assessing his place in the organization, over the long haul. Understand?"

"Yes, Comrade I understand and you can always count on my unwavering support. "

"Yes, that is true; you have always been there for me and I will go to my grave thanking every god there is for bringing you to my side. No man could have a greater friend. Thank you, friend."

Jet was truly humbled by the president's words. What was there to say? His mind raced for proper words but all he could do was look into president's eyes and say, "Thank you Yanlin, nothing means more to me or ever will than your enduring trust."

With a tear almost coming to his eyes he quickly asked, "When will the rest of the group arrive?"

"The meeting shall commence in three hours at five. My initial presentation won't take long and then I have a special dinner planned so we can all relax and be ready for tomorrow which will be a full day. I have a Russian delegation coming and must be back in my office by noon on Monday the 29th, so we will need to finish up tomorrow without fail."

Jet nodded understanding and rising said, "I will leave you to your preparations and be back here before five." The president nodded and selected a file from the four files that were the only things on the massive desk, turned his chair around and gazed out at his beautiful underground landscape. Orchid plants were in profusion and their delicate stems sported blossoms of every color and hue. Pushing a button on a remote control, the glass wall, behind the desk, slid away and the sounds of the waterfall washed away the thoughts of the day. He just sat there, for the longest time, soaking in the sounds and beauty, knowing that soon, very soon he would replace the American president as the most powerful leader on earth.

CHAPTER
3

The participants, i.e. (the Group of Five) were all seated around a large oval table in conference room one, which had a private door to the president's office. It was one minute to the hour when the private door opened, and the supreme leader of the People's Republic of China entered the room. His four comrades immediately rose from their seats and came to attention, not military attention, but high respect attention and the president took note.

President Hu seated himself at the table, but not before he circled the oval shaking hands and making small talk with each of the four men that he had hand selected, out of a country of 1.371 billion.

"Before we get to the meat of today's meeting, I wish to sincerely thank each of you for your participation in the Rainbow Zhanlue. I am sure you will all agree that the actions we took back in November of 1998 were historical; no, monumental in terms of our present day position in the world of nations. When we started a 'Made in China' label had the worldwide reputation of being a shabby inferior product that would have a short life. Today you can be in any city in the world and if the bar code starts with 690 through 695, you know that item was Made in China and that it is a quality product. From Gucci bags to Apple computers, 'Made in China' is a positive for most world shoppers. We did that! We changed the concept, and that change has been a total positive for our workers. It has raised the standard of living for the average citizen and we are responsible. So, I thank you from the bottom of my heart for your hard work and dedication." President Hu stood and directed his attention to each man around the table as he softly clapped his hands. It was a true and deeply moving tribute and each man was humbled to be in the President's presence.

Re-seating himself with his piercing black eyes moving from man to man, he said in a soft but strong voice, "Before we start let us remember our comrades Yide Du and Fan Chang Long who would be here with us today had they not departed earth for their place in our ancestral world. They were true patriots and we were privileged to call them comrades. What I am going to ask you today is light-years ahead, and a thousand times more important that what we were able to accomplish over the last seventeen years." He stopped and let his words sink into each of the concentrating heads that faced him. "Yes, what we do today will shape the course of world events like nothing ever has. Buddha, Christ and Muhammad were all earth-changing events, but they will all pale when compared to the impact that our new Zhanlue will have on world history. Once initiated, life on earth will never again be the same, so we need strong hearts and resolution of the highest caliber to ensure that we are successful."

Pausing for a long slow drink of water, he noted the level of attention around the table was high, each face was concentrating and hanging on every word and he could tell that their interest was peaked and the anticipation level was incredibly high.

"I have named this new project and I shall speak the words just once and then from now until the end of time they shall never be spoken again, not by me and not by any of you. None of your underlings, nor for that fact, no one in the world outside this room will ever know. Do I have your solemn oath?"

Each head nodded in the affirmative as the President made eye contact with each member.

"Very well, the code designation is DBZ and it stands for Dragon Breath Zhanlue. It is a new form of warfare and when we have inflicted it on the rest of the world the Yuan will be the world's standard currency, we will control world commerce and we will be the most influential and powerful country on the face of the earth. Our reign will last for thousands of years, if not for all time. Our Chinese ancestors, thousands of years from now, will know our names and will be grateful that they had forefathers with such foresight and initiative."

"So, my loyal Comrades you now know the goals and I am sure you can each appreciate the importance of our new mission. You may be asking yourself why is this Zhanlue is so important at this particular point in time and I will explain. If you have been following the news from America you know that just ten days ago an outsider, a person with no previous government or political experience announced he was running for president of the United States. The current field is large as there are now seventeen candidates. We had been hoping that Jeb Bush, the former President's son and/or brother would be the obvious Republican candidate and that if he won, we could have normal relations like we did with the previous Bush administrations. We, like the rest of the world, also assume that Hillary Clinton will be the democratic candidate and we want her to win so we can return to the Clinton days, which was a time when we made tremendous inroads. This newcomer, Donald J. Trump is a millionaire businessman and the dossier we have on him leads us to believe that he would try to reign in our expansion and that he would be very difficult to deal with. If, by some strange chance he won we could look forward to strained relationships, at the least and all out war at the worst. He is a fighter and he will not allow us to continue down the road we have been traveling. To protect our current position in today's global order, we must do everything we can do to defeat him and I have committed my special presidential funds to this purpose."

Looking around the room he asked, "Questions so far?"

Jet How cocked his head, looked over his glasses and asked, "Since you undoubtedly believe that this one man poses a threat to our global position and our goals, to dominate world affairs, why don't we just expunge him? Accidents happen every day."

"Yes, that is one solution, but I doubt we could insulate our regime from culpability, but that, of course, is the ultimate solution and should all else fail it will remain on the table. Anyone else?"

"If not let me expand further on the process details so that you will have an overall picture of the total Zhanlue." Now standing, looking, down at his outline he continued. "Job one will be to disrupt Trumps candidacy. Jet will be in charge and if you have ideas or inside knowledge, feed it to him. Trump has had a colorful past and we can use his indiscretions against him. Put any of the American and European mainline media people you can on the payroll and make the incentives worthwhile for the journalists you select. Use our ambassador in Washington to bring the current administration's agency heads to the table and encourage them to investigate the Trump campaign ties to Russia. Let it be known that our government may have information that links Russia to the Trump campaign and try to compromise all Trump campaign staffers into some kind of Russian collusion. I have heard from the Ambassador that there may also be a link to Ukraine so let your research expand into all the Russian satellite countries as well."

Returning to his seat the President ask. "Questions Jet?"

"No, I understand the goal and I will organize a staff and start the ball rolling. We have many student-agents working in the universities around America and I shall get them organized into an anti-Trump movement which, with all the current unrest, should be a relatively easy task."

"Lin, (Lin Wong First Minister of Economics and Trade) I want you to concentrate on getting as many American Pharmacology and Medical manufacturing companies to relocate their operations to China as quickly as possible. Offer the big American drug and equipment manufacturers money-losing incentives, if necessary, to relocate their manufacturing plants to China. Your goal is to get as many health-related companies to make their products in China as possible."

Looking around the room he smiled and added, "If a worldwide medical pandemic should happen to strike, we want to ensure that a vast majority of the world's countries critical supplies like drugs, medicine, medical equipment and medical supplies come from China. If a hospital in Atlanta, Georgia needs critical supplies and or medical apparatus we want them to have to buy the items from China. This is critical to the overall Zhanlue, so set up a special operation to do nothing but solicit medical equipment, supplies and drugs. For example, would it not be interesting if the west woke up in a worldwide crisis, and discovered that large percentages of antibiotics could only be sourced from Chinese companies or foreign companies in China, that we control, with regard to their access to raw materials and labor." The President's smile was diabolical and Lin Wong understood his mission but for clarity asked, "Comrade President what is my budget for this phase of the operation?"

"One- hundred million American dollars to start and if you need more let me know. By 2019 I want China to be the world's largest supplier of pharmaceutical, medical equipment and medical supplies."

Pausing, the President refilled his water glass and observed, "You may have noted that I have no assistants present nor will I during the course of these DBZ meetings. There will be no written record and your assignments will not be detailed, as is normal practice. We will all work from memory and if you need authorization for money transfers, etc., just let me know and I will initiate the required paperwork with justifications that I will fabricate."

Turning to Admiral Cheng Wanguan the President inquired, "Admiral Cheng, do I recall correctly that your roots were in the countryside, specifically the Guangdong area?"

"Yes, Comrade President that is correct, but I left the area early and only return to visit some of my wife's relatives that are still area farmers."

"Well, I am going to ask you to step back in time and establish working connections with the agriculture giants of China and America."

"And what is my goal Comrade President?"

"The goal is for China, over the next few years, to become a major food supplier to the world. We have over 300 million farmers and we want productivity to increase by at least fifteen percent, which will be difficult but automation in the rice industry, similar to what goes on in Northern California, will help and that will mean major restructuring of rice growing areas. We want to become competitive in wheat, tobacco, potatoes, peanuts, soybeans, corn, tea, oil seeds, pork, and fish. By controlling the world's supply of medical items as well as a big portion of the food chain we will be better able to control foreign populations. Questions?"

The Admiral had sunk lower and lower in his chair trying to keep up with what the President was explaining and he wondered if this was some kind of test. All Chinese leaders worry about being tested and missing the mark which meant loss of privilege, loss of the lifestyle and maybe loss of life. The Admiral developed survival skills over years and years of careful and selective support and his gut told him this was just another test in the many that he had passed. Back to reality the Admiral puffed up, as had been his leadership style of twenty years and replied in a cool and straight-forward manner, "Yes, Comrade President, I see where you want to be and I will use all of my energy and talent to get us there. It is a truly ambitious goal, but I will organize a staff that will be able to cover all aspects of your requirements. Will the minister of agriculture be in my loop or is this to be outside his area of responsibility?"

"Comrade, just explain to the minister the goals I have outlined, tell him that you are a special presidential appointment to aid him in achieving these goals and, if you wish, we can have a three-way meeting so that he understands you are the President's messenger. Do you think that will give you the cover you need?"

"Yes, Comrade President, that is exactly what is required and may I say I never cease to be amazed at the way you can foresee situations and be ready with the necessary action."

"Thank you Admiral. I look forward to working with you and the minister on this project. By the way, I am available to you all on a twenty-four seven basis. Makes no difference when you call or e-mail, but please prefix your communication with the code letters, so I know it has a critical timeline and is not routine business."

Before the President could continue Jet asked, "Comrade President would it be better to just have a code word we could use rather than the designation?"

"I see where you are going Jet. Maybe that would be prudent to have an alternative code. Let's think on it and tomorrow before we adjourn we will make a decision. For now, I think we have earned a nice dinner and the staff has gone all out to ensure a meal that will be remembered. I will see you all in the private dining room by seven thirty. Come earlier if you wish to have a cocktail before dinner. Meeting adjourned."

CHAPTER
4

The Friday morning meeting started promptly at nine with the same cast of characters present; all clear-headed and ready for the final session that would, each hoped, explain why the President thought this was such an earth-shaking Zhanlue. He had explained that stopping Trump was a primary goal, but that did not add up to changing the world for thousands of years to come and none of the participants had been able to connect the dots and, of course, that is exactly what the Supreme President of China anticipated. He was not the leader of over 1.3 billion people by chance. He was not only extremely intelligent, but had a clever, devious mind that had allowed him to manipulate superiors and underlings alike, so as to extract from them exactly what he wanted and his wants could only be described as gargantuan.

Looking around the table the leader asks, "Did you enjoy the special dinner last night?" All replied enthusiastically in the positive with words of praise and thanks.

Looking at Jet the President reminisced, "I never cease to be amazed at the Peking duck presentation. I have seen it a thousand times and still the anticipation is almost breathtaking."

Admiral Cheng jumped into the conversation by asking, "How do the cooks do that? It is culinary magic to watch the paltered duck be set in the middle of the table, all puffed up like some of those pompous Europeans in their fancy uniforms, and then with the lightest stroke of an ivory chopstick, down the breastbone, the duck puffs up and falls open to expose the rice stuffing and vegetables. It is like a miniature explosion. One grain more or less of rice and it would not work."

The President smiled at the enthusiasm generated by the Admiral's replay and said, "What more is to be said after that elegant description? I can almost smell the delicious aromas, from just your description Admiral. And now to business. I can sense that you all are wondering how interfering in the American election can be an earth-changing Zhanlue, but that is just the tip of the iceberg."

Looking around to insure himself of complete security, he said in a slow measured cadence, "Yes, that is just the tip of the iceberg. Follow me closely comrades as I am not prepared to say this more than once. Should Mr. Trump be elected he will try to disrupt our current operational modem and if he succeeds, we will have some very difficult years. If he is elected, we will use the Russian/ Ukraine collusion stories, and pull every string of every democratic opponent. We will enlist the aid of the heads of agencies that I have been courting during all the Obama years and we will do everything we can, for the full four years of his presidency, to get him impeached. That is the word the Americans use to describe replacing leadership; it's known as an outright coup in every other country on the face of the planet."

Pausing briefly, he continued with all eyes riveted on him and all brains making rapid and likely scenarios. "Prior to the 2020 election, in late 2019 or very early in 2020 we shall release our Dragon Breath on the peoples of the world. Millions around the planet will die, including hundreds of thousands in America and Mr. Trump's presidency will be over. He cannot weather what we will unleash on him. The people will rise up and most likely some old Democratic white man will convince the masses that he can lead them out of the pandemic. This pandemic will be triggered by a virus that we are currently developing at a secret lab in one of our outlying cities, but that will change. I am in the process of building an ultra-secret lab far out in the western dry lands and it will be completed within a few months. We will then transfer the research to this new lab which will be the ultimate in medical technology and security. We will select an outlying city to be the source of the virus and that will require sacrificing many of our citizens but it is no different than war, and sending troops off into battle. Yes, we may lose a million people, but we would be prepared to lose that many in any conventional war and of course more in a nuclear war."

Pausing again for a sip of water he quickly continued. "The plan will be to infect several thousand people, people who already have travel plans to Italy, or Europe, or New York, or South America. Within a week the virus will be in every capital of the world and will spread like wildfire. Millions will die, economies will shut down and we will dole out medical supplies after we, of course, take care of our own first. Food supplies will go short and there will be worldwide panic and we will be the masters that the world will look to for help. We of course will have a vaccine available but will not release it to the world until their economies are in shambles and then we shall ride in and take charge and within a few decades most people around the world will be speaking Chinese, spending the world currency know as yuan and buying Chinese medicines, supplies and food. I predict that within twenty-five years there will be one worldwide government run from Beijing and we will not have dropped one atomic bomb. In all of this the World Health Organization will be our partner, backing up our claims and declaring that it was America and the Trump regime that started the worldwide pandemic. The W.H.O. will follow our lead because we have been greasing the palms of their entire leadership for the last few years and we shall continue to do so in the future."

Looking at Four Star General Zhao Keshi the President asked, "General your part of the Zhanlue is to make certain that our Armed Forces have the capability to be nation builders. An army that can go anywhere in the world, on short notice, and take control of entire countries. An organizational nightmare I am sure, but you will develop teams that can run governments and keep the populations under control, no matter what level of force may be required. Do you understand your mission?"

The General, his dark sharp Mongolian features in total concentration, cocked his head and replied, "Comrade President, I can see the need, I can understand the importance to the overall Zhanlue and I will develop plans to cover every country and every contingency." Before the President could reply the General continued, "I will develop plans starting with America and working through the European continent, with all the lesser South American and African countries to follow. With regard to our Asian neighbors would you anticipate they need to be near the top of the list or can we wait until America and Europe are neutralized?"

"And that comrade is why I chose the General to be on this team. Straight to the point, good questions that I shall answer in due time. Thank you General. Do you wish to add anything at this time?"

"Yes, Comrade I am certain that we have ministers that currently have such responsibilities and I would like to be able to use that brain trust to proof our plans and suggestions."

"By all means General and I shall work up a list of people that you can contact on a continuing basis and your budget will be one hundred million, so do not be concerned that this will have an impact on your current operating budget."

The General nodded understanding.

"Well Comrades that covers the assignments for each of you. As questions come to mind, please e-mail or by secure messenger let me have your thoughts and/or questions. A timeline world be appreciated within the next sixty days. Unless otherwise advised, I will assume that you will meet that deadline. Let's say by August 30, and in all your communications use the code word Tiger."

Jet How almost came off his chair as he could not contain himself and almost shouted, "Of course, the Dragon and the Tiger! In our Chinese martial arts, 'Dragon Style' in used to describe a style of fighting based on understanding and movement while 'Tiger Style' is based on brute strength and memorization of techniques. Simply brilliant Comrade President, simply brilliant, but we would expect no less from our Supreme leader." Everyone at the table stood and clapped softly for their leader.

"Thank you, comrades. Thank you for your confidence and I do not want you to think that I have given you tough assignments without giving myself a special project. As I mentioned earlier within a few months the new desert research complex will be fully functional. It is located in the Nei Monggoi Zizhique desert near the city of Minquin and it will be a state of the art biologically research center staffed by the most eminent and accomplished scientific minds that our country has to offer. You need not know any further details, but let me say it will be the most sensitive installation in all of China and its existence will only be known to a handful of our top research scientists. It will be where the final form of the virus will be developed and where the vaccines, that we may ALL need someday, will be stored." Jet How quickly asked, "What about the research center in Wuhan?"

"It shall remain as our Trojan Horse," the President said with a sly evil smile.

Standing up President Hu announced in low and humble manner his thanks for each member's participation and further noted that their next meeting would be on Friday, July 24, which would be the third quarter moon, which he had always believed was his personal time of good luck.

CHAPTER
5

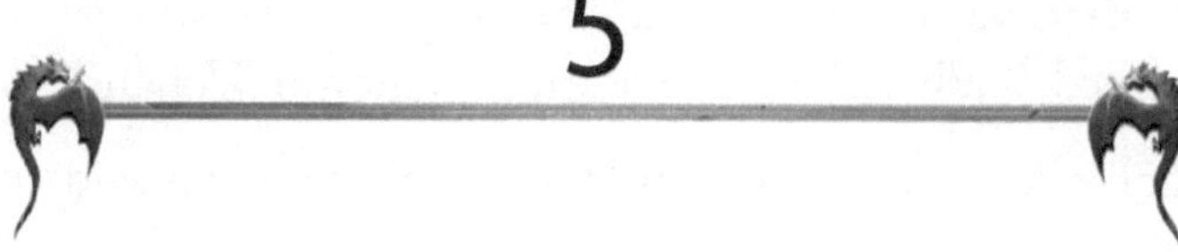

All the President's guests had departed, with spinning heads, leaving President Hu to enjoy his private complex in peace and quiet. He loved sitting in the area outside his office listening to the waterfall and enjoying the beauty of the immaculately tended gardens. It was where he did his best long-range thinking. Away from family, friends and his hectic office, where he would have to be Monday to take care of the every growing stack of presidential requirements.

He called the complex he was building, in the Western desert, Chaoxue (Chinese for lair), and his mind kept roving the details, over and over again to make sure he had not missed any important element.

Only six months ago he had sent out teams, to the construction site he had personally selected, disguised as oil and gas exploration units. They roamed an area of desert scrub land that backed up to a steep mountain range drilling test bores at specific locations. The American satellites, that scanned the Chinese landscape every day, did not miss the activity, but it was soon ignored as just another routine quest for the lifeblood liquid that fueled the planets engines. In reality the holes drilled into the wind-swept plateau were only ten meters deep by fifteen centimeters in diameter and into each hole a steel pipe filled with concrete was installed. The threaded pipe stub only extended above the surface by thirty centimeters (about 12 inches) and each stub was camouflaged by rocks and plants so as to be undetectable from the air. The hole pattern covered an area the size of a soccer field and extended right up to the mountain's edge.

When the over five hundred stubs were in place the drilling teams moved ten kilometers to the east and pretended to drill additional holes for the next thirty days, just part of the intricate ruse to foil any chance observations from the eyes in the sky.

On the next moon-less night, after the pipe installation job had been completed, and as the sun was setting over the arid alluvial plane, almost ten thousand Army special forces troops moved on to the stub site. They arrived in military helicopters from surrounding bases, some as far as two hundred kilometers away. Each unit was assigned twenty stubs and within minutes of landing six-meter steel pipes were mated to each stub and heavy gauge wire was strung from the top of each pole to its neighbor. Within three hours all the pipes were in place, each connected by wire and the process of hanging camouflage netting was underway. By three a.m. the soccer field area was under a complete netting roof that had been designed to blend into the existing countryside. It was a marvel of engineering technology as high-altitude photos, taken by the Chinese Air force, the following morning, could not detect the camouflage area from the surrounding land. The President had studied the photos from the day before and from the day after and even with a magnification glass he could not see where the netting started or stopped. Back at his headquarters in Beijing, President Hu called the special forces General Jen Maxiaotian and congratulated him on a job well done and asked, "When will phase two commence?"

"Tomorrow night the machinery will be moved under the netting at each end of the camouflage area, next to the mountain, and within three days the components shall all be assembled, and the units will start boring into the mountain side."

"Thank you General and let me know when the tunneling has actually gotten underway, and General also let me know how many meters the units can bore per twenty-four hours, as soon as that data becomes available."

"Yes, I shall be in touch Comrade President."

President Hu sat back in his chair and stared at the stain glass windows that cover the ceiling of his office and envisioned the remaining requirements until the job was completed. He was looking for problem areas but nothing critical seemed to be on the horizon. In his mind's eye, he envisioned the two great boring machines that would soon be attacking the hillsides under the netting. Each machine was capable of boring a ten-meter circular tunnel into the mountains side. One of the giants would start at the east end and the other at the west end of the netting and they would eventually come together having created a "U" shaped underground cavern. The total length of the bore would be over three-hundred meters. At that point they would back down to where the curve of the "U" started and then bore straight into the mountain another hundred meters with the final configuration being like the letter "H" with the crossbar having a slight radius. The top of the "H" would be where the machines would stay for the rest of time as once they finished the digging their large motors would run generators that would provide power to the facility. At the very back of the two tunnels, at the deepest point of penetration, thick rubber butyl liners, ten-thousand-gallon capacity, would be installed to act as reservoirs for water, fuel and waste. Before the bladders would be installed vent holes would be drilled in the ceiling and large capacity blowers would be installed that would bring fresh air to the complex. The vents would, of course, be camouflaged and filtered and piping would be run from the storage areas to utility terminals located near each entrance.

As the cuts into the mountain proceeded, all the waste dirt and rock would be spread out under the netting so that there would be no tailing piles. All the area under the netting would eventually be covered with the fill material and native plants would be planted following detailed maps of the area prior to any construction, so that the netting could be removed as it did not have a life span of more than a year or two as the desert winds howled through this part of the desert with a vengeance.

Once the tunnels were completed and the boring machines were in their final resting place, the tunnel walls and ceiling would be lined with prefabricated plastic panels. The curved panels were two meters wide and on the back side of each were utility lines for compressed air, cooling and heating, water, sewer, disinfectant and electrical lines complete with outlets. Each panel was locked to its neighbor with latches on the back side and all mating surfaces were tongue and groove with medical grade rubber seals to ensure air and watertight connections.

Starting from the back the panels were locked together, all connections made and then a concrete pad was laid down on the floor which was covered with gleaming white tile. The floor had a built-in drainage system so the entire complex could be disinfected and cleaned. It only took twenty-five days after the digging had stopped to get all the utilities, panels and flooring system installed, but then almost anything can be done quickly, if labor and cost of material are no factor and the Supreme President is running the operation.

By mid-July the major construction was complete, the laboratory equipment had been installed along with wall partitions that formed the various offices, labs. cafeteria and sleeping quarters. The west tunnel became the entrance, and the east tunnel became the exit. The scientists, doctors and laboratory workers would arrive at the west tunnel, clear security (a small chip inserted in each person's left ear lobe obviated the need for identification cards, etc.) and enter the complex through a steel airlock door system. There they would strip down, deposit their clothes in red bags that would be incinerated, shower, have medical examinations and then dress for work in full disposable protective gear. Their shift lasted for seven days and at the end of the week the workers would exit the east tunnel after having showered and spent several hours in a ultraviolet disinfectant room. They dressed out in new clothing, had an exit medical exam and then boarded their bus for the nighttime ride back to an air base ninety kilometers away. There were two teams of scientists, forty in each team and thirty-five full time security, maintenance workers including cooks and stewards, who were all Chinese Army Special Forces. Each army member would put in thirty-day tours at the facility.

The updates from General Maxiaotian were encouraging and the president could not have been more pleased with the operation that would be going online come July 20, which was only five days away. The Group of Five next meeting would be on July 24, and the President could not be more pleased that he would be able to tell them that the Chaoxue facility was up and running. Looking back on the last thirty days the President had to admit that everyone in the chain had done outstanding work and he was perplexed as to how to properly say thank you, which was not needed, but which was his leadership style. A personnel visit coupled with performance awards would go a long way toward thanking the workers and anyway he wanted to tour the complex before they started transferring in the dozens of virus strains, that had been developed at the Wuhan lab.

CHAPTER
6

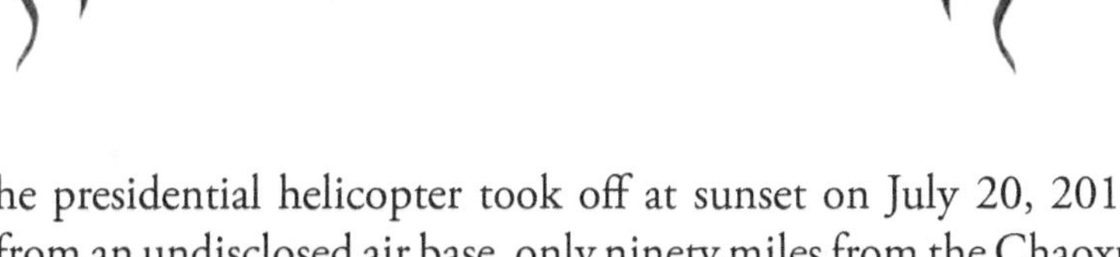

The presidential helicopter took off at sunset on July 20, 2015, from an undisclosed air base, only ninety miles from the Chaoxue lab, and just forty-three minutes later landed outside the netting, near the west side entrance, in a cloud of dust. The pilot shut down the main rotor, and waited to open the door until the dust was cleared away by the ever-present wind that howled across the landscape.

Only two men exited the craft, the President of China and Jet How Chung. They were greeted by just one man who quickly ushered them across the desert sand, under the netting and through the main steel entry doors. The two visitors found themselves in a brightly lit bare room, with a thick glass panel barring any further entry. The escort slicked back his long black hair and said, "Comrade President it is good to see you again. Sorry about the dust and the wind, it's just part of the landscape."

"No problem Director Yang, we totally understand and no apologies are necessary." Looking around the President smiled and asked, "Are we allowed any further into your Chaoxue?"

"Of course comrade, this way please." If by magic the glass panel rose straight up, and the three men walked into an area that was separated into two compartments with signs that directed men to the left side and women to the right. Director Yang entered the compartment labeled "men" and the President and Jet followed along. The director started his briefing, "At this point all clothes and foot coverings are removed and deposited in the red barrel, to be burned later. The workers then proceed into a bank of showers that are activated when they walk through the shower compartment. On the other side they dry, and doctors are waiting to give them a complete physical including temperature and blood pressure checks, and then they proceed to the dressing room where they don surgical scrub clothing, which they change each day, and the clothing is cleaned in our own laundry facilities which are located near the generators and utility equipment." The President and Jet absorbed the narrative with bobbing heads. "Before we proceed any further would you mind putting these protective booties, over your shoes, and wearing these face masks so we can proceed farther into the complex?"

Compliance was immediate and Director Yang cautioned, "From here to the exit are sleeping quarters, labs, a cafeteria, meeting rooms, a workout gym, game room and storage vaults. The assistant director and I have the only vault combinations and these walk-in vaults are where we store all finished work and all work in process. Any questions?"

"What form does the work week take?" Jet inquired.

"All workers from the outside are here for seven days, then four days at their home and then seven on again. During each twenty-four hour period the maximum work time is ten hours, and that rule will be strictly enforced. Workers are forbidden to discuss their work activities with other workers not in their particular team. We have divided the workers into six person teams and those workers can discuss work with each other, but only in controlled and monitored meeting rooms. Work-related matters cannot be discussed in any other of the complex venues other than the actual working labs. Each team has their own lab and meeting room and no one person other than myself and the assistant director know what the different teams are working on or toward."

"Director Yang," the President said in a commanding voice, "I would like to have a one-page profile on each person, including you and your assistant. Please have that transmitted to Jet at the address he will give you under top secret priority protocols. You, Comrade are to communicate only with Jet, relative to the progress of your work. Ordering supplies and all the required activities to keep this operation at the top of its game can proceed with the Health Minister, but I caution you, not one word of your research data can be shared with anyone but Jet and myself. " Looking blue-black daggers at the Director, the President asked in a soft voice, "Do I have your complete understanding Comrade Director?"

Director Yang felt beads of sweat cover his brow and he replied, "Yes, Comrade President I understand the reporting requirements and you may be certain I shall follow your directions to the letter."

"Thank you Director. Can I assume that the balance of the complex is similar to what we have seen?"

"Yes Comrade, and I am prepared to show you every detail, but yes, it is just more of the same."

"Well Jet, if you will give the Director your top secret contact details I think we can be on our way, but before departing I want to once again remind the Director that this project is bigger than any one person. If any of your rules of employment are breached, no matter how small, it is your duty to the state, to provide Comrade Chung with the factual details. If a breach is not reported and later discovered you, Director Yang will be held responsible and you, your family and any living blood will disappear from this planet. You, Comrade must instill that understanding to your employees. From time to time Jet shall tell you the name of a person that will be joining your teams and that person may or may not be a known scientists, but he or she will be welcomed into your group. Is all of the above crystal clear?"

Director Yang knew from the tips of his toes to twitching end of his Roman nose that his very existence was hanging in the balance and in a soft almost whispered reply he said, "Yes, Comrade President I understand and shall guide this entity with your words imprinted in my skull."

The President smiled at his companions as the three men moved back toward the entrance, leaving their booties and masks in the red barrel. No one shook hands, the President and Jet just nodded to the Director and disappeared out the steel entry door, and fought the wind as they made their way to the waiting helicopter.

Once airborne Jet asked, "Do you think the Director will last?"

"Hard to say, old friend, but I am sure you will test him often."

"Yes, Comrade President you can count on that." Pausing, Jet continued, "Have you ever looked into what America has given to us over the years?"

"No, but I do have some recollection of hearing fringe details, but I am sure you are going to give me all the details, as is your usual habit."

Smiling at the President, Jet said, "Yes, I think it is important and I think it will help us all understand just how far we can push your Zhanlue. They, the Americans, do not think like we do and that is important when we are going to be so heavily involved in their politics and economy. To improve understanding, it all started in 1940 when President Roosevelt gave China 25 million US dollars and directed that they use the money to buy pursuit aircraft. Of course, such a loan directly benefited the huge aircraft makers and helped cement the President's power base. In the years after the war millions of American taxpayer dollars flowed to China to help compensate for the losses we suffered during the war. I saw a figure that over 14 million Chinese died during W.W.II and somehow the American mind thought that money would help China recover from that loss, never mind that we looked at it as 14 million less mouths to feed, but such is the western thinking." Smiling his diabolical smile Jet continued, "As an example in 1999 we received 2.4 billion, in 2001 we received only 1.4 billion and this past year we are down into the millions, but it is still substantial, but we too are starting to give the struggling countries aid and someday we may buy as much influence in the third world as does America."

President Hu interrupted and said, "You best finish up this class, my teacher, as we are just a few minutes from landing and I have a full schedule."

"Yes, I will finish up with one recent bit of information that you may know, but bears repeating, We can thank the Obama regime for helping us fund the lab at Wuhan to the tune of 3.7 million dollars. It is all tied to the World Health Organization and my guess is that if Hillary is elected we can continue to see this kind of investment on the part of the American intellectuals and their misguided, but appreciated, 'deeds to help mankind', a misguided and naive attitude, but one that makes me smile."

"Yes, I smile too and I thank you for the lesson. I am looking forward to seeing you at the meeting on July 24."

The helicopter kissed the tarmac, with a soft scuff, as the President's limo pulled up next to the aircraft, with Jet's limo bringing up the rear. Before deplaning, the President shook Jet's hand and said, "This would not be nearly so much fun without you. Stay well old friend."

Smiling from ear to ear, Jet replied, "Thank you Comrade President, I shall do my best."

CHAPTER
7

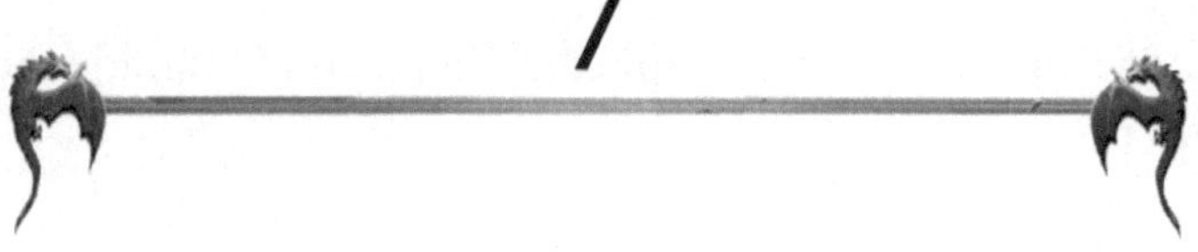

"Jet, let the record you are keeping show that the second meeting of the Group of Five has commenced this date, July 24, 2015, with all members present."

"Yes, Comrade President, so noted."

"Comrades, a few days ago, Jet and I toured the complex we are calling Chaoxue, and I am pleased to report that the new secret laboratory facility is fully staffed and functional. The new Director is one of the world's leading authorities in the area of disease control and he has the full support of the World Health Organization; however, we have asked him to keep a low profile as there is no need for us to advertise our capabilities. Since our meeting a month ago, I would like to hear what progress each of you have been making. If you have run into road blocks let me know and Jet and I will look into clearing the jam. Jet, tell us what you can about the political situation in America."

"Thank you Comrade." Standing, Jet spoke without notes and immediately got everyone's attention by saying, "You may think me crazy, old and senile, but I have been reviewing the political scene in America and I am certain that come the nominating convention in Cleveland, on July 21, 2016, less than a year away, that Donald Trump will in fact be the Republican candidate. He will out work, out fox and out perform the other sixteen contenders and the American public will rally to his brash, unpredictable style of campaigning." Jet let his prognosis sink in and then continued with renewed vigor, "The question then comes, can Trump beat Hillary Clinton, and as of today the poles and public opinion are solidly in her court. In fact, some are predicting she will run away with the election, as she will be the first female presidential candidate, and the female voting block, in America, makes up about fifty- five percent of the total. I am not yet prepared to call that race, but I am prepared to tell you that the organizations we are putting together in America will have just one purpose and that is to defeat Donald Trump. Questions?"

President Hu looked at his old friend and asked, "Where do you get all the energy, are you taking some secret drug?" The group erupted in laughter and Jet gave his comrade a snappy salute and returned to his chair.

The President looked around the table and commented, "I hope the rest of you are on the same drug. Now let's hear from Comrade Wong. What say you Lin?"

Lin Wong stood up and looked at his comrades' faces and with a dead-pan expression and asked, "Jet has not seen fit to share his drugs with me, but I am truly excited about the progress my team has made and I am happy to share the details with you. As you know, in the simplest form, my mission is to capture the health care supply market in America, without their realizing what is happening. China will become the pharmaceutical supply house, not only to America, but to the world and of course, that means we will be in the catbird seat should a pandemic strike the planet. So far, it has been a simple process of identifying every company in China that has a health care related product, from simple band-aids to hospital beds, ventilators and drugs. We have cataloged these companies and divided them into five teams, based on the primary sub-groupings in the overall health care industry. We then took listings from Dun and Bradstreet reports that list the top two-hundred healthcare companies in America by sales and net assets. It was simple to match our Chinese companies with the top manufacturing companies in America and once the match was made, we asked the Chinese companies to go to America, find their counterpart and attempt to either buy the company or transfer a portion of their production to a new plant that we would help them build in China. We, of course, underwrote the cost of the travel and subsistence and we will, of course, help with the financing required. As we speak, we have over one hundred Chinese Health Care executives in

America beating the bushes for American companies that want to make high profits by sourcing their supply chain from Chinese factories. I expect by year end that over five-hundred Chinese businessmen will have been in America and that new factories will start materializing in every region of China, and that our percentage of the health care supply chain will go to dramatic levels."

Looking around at his comrades he asked, "Questions?"

As usual, Jet cut to the chase and asked, "And how much will this cost? Seems to me that buying one major company could blow the 100 million that we have budgeted for your operation."

"Yes, Comrade you are correct, but I have talked to the Minister of Finance and if we find a large expensive company we will treat it as an individual development project and I am told that funds can be made available, in that we currently control just a little bit less than one trillion dollars of America's debt."

"Thank you Comrade, a fine report and your aggressive action is something that I truly admire and appreciate."

"You are welcome, Comrade President."

"Well General Yang, what do you have for us today?"

The General rose from his chair and was an impressive site in his full dress uniform with a chest full of medals and ribbons. He was just over six feet tall, of Mongolian descent and looked like he could chew up railroad spikes and spit them at you. "Thank you Comrade President, and I wish that my report was as progressive and upbeat as my colleagues' but the Army moves in slow motion sometimes and I don't have a great deal to report, but we have started on the project and we are making good progress. As you know, I need to have units available at a minute's notice, that can go anywhere in the world and take over all operational aspects of running a country. Everything from fighting off unfriendly neighbors or developed countries that think they are the policemen of the world, as well as all the infrastructure elements of running a society. Armies are not usually given such responsibilities. Usually we go in, smash the enemy and turn the reigns of power over to the civilian part of the government, providing only support and security. Since you are asking us to be smasher and nursemaid, it is a challenge that my people must wrap their heads around. We are developing detailed operational plans and are using one South American country, one African country and one Asian country as our models. In other words, the model we develop for, say the South American country of Bolivia, will be a standard we can use for any other country in that hemisphere. Right now, we have set up a curriculum for all major ranking officers and for the top ranks of the non-officer grades, and the schooling involves every aspect of running state and local governments. In addition, we have language classes in over twenty-five major dialectics, so that we will be able to communicate with the locals, no matter the location. So, you see there is not much brick and mortar at this point in time; however, we are engaging with the air force to come up with systems to facilitate heavy lifts of men and machinery, to any corner of the globe. In summary, I think the upper grades of our military forces can see the end game, but the further down the ranks you go it is apparent that there is little comprehension of the overall mission and of course we cannot explain the long game, so it is a challenge to say the least. Questions?"

Jet again jumped into the breach and asked, "General, since you will never be able to explain the mission fully, until an actual crisis has developed, and we must seize control of a country, do you think that the training might be diluted by the unknown?"

"Exactly, Comrade. It is a difficult sell at this time but as I have heard you say, 'Impossible dreams become a reality when given space and time'."

"Thank you General, it will be interesting to watch this develop and if any of you have ideas that may help the General be sure you share. This is a team effort and working together we will conquer, working alone we will fail."

The General acknowledged the President's remarks with a nod.

"Last but not least, tell us Admiral Wanguan how you have been attacking your part of the problem?"

"Thank you Comrade President," the Admiral said as he rose from his seat to address the group.

"Comrades, feeding our people today is a challenge; feeding the world even at reduced population levels is going to be the ultimate challenge, and I think we should be prepared to see the world population decline by as much as thirty percent. That may seem a ghoulash projection, but in reality it may be the ultimate solution. Right now, the world population is estimated at 7.341 billion and a thirty percent reduction would bring it down to about 5.2 billion, which is almost exactly the number of humans that walked the planet in 1995. My team is looking into all the ways you can imagine to increase food production from automation to extensive fish and algae farms, which will provide the protein levels the populous will require. Almost every country has marginal lands that are not being utilized and these technologies are adaptable to marginal land, with good engineering. A worldwide pandemic would trigger a drop in oil prices, we would see thousands of restaurants cease to exist and would put vacation destinations and their economies into a free fall. I cannot give you specifics at this point, but we have teams of some of the best and brightest working on ways to feed starving populations, but there is a plus side and that is a population that is hungry can be controlled by masters with food. We are crunching the numbers and looking into every imaginable dream and at our next meeting I promise to have more specific data. Questions?"

President Hu stood up, which signaled the meeting was about over and stated, "Thank you all for your thoughtful presentations. Our next meeting will be Wednesday September 23, at nine a.m. I shall be looking for more specific recommendations and at that point we will know if we have to worry about Mr. Trump being elected. There are sixteen other candidates so maybe we will dodge the Trump bullet. Have a nice weekend and thank you again for your participation. Meeting adjourned."

An hour later President Hu was sitting at his desk, drinking in the outside views and sounds when the Presidents aide softly said, "Sir, Comrade Jet wonders if you have a few minutes before you depart for Beijing?"

"Tell him yes and send him in."

"Yes sir."

The President's door opened and Jet stuck his head around the corner and asked, "Have a few minutes Yanlin?"

"Of course, what's on your mind?"

"As you know, I have strong opinions on how the American election will go and I just have a deep down gut feeling that the Republican candidate will be Trump, and that regardless of the last minute polls, which will show Hillary on top, it will be the upset of their 240 year history. I talked to grass root people all over America and there is an unrest that is bubbling to the surface. They don't like globalize and they want America on top; it's almost like a competitive sporting event. At any rate I wanted to give you my insight and let you know that I shall never work so hard to prove I'm wrong."

"I have been thinking about that Jet and I think you might want to think about an insurance policy."

"Insurance policy, I don't understand."

"Let us say your gut is right and that Trump is elected. He cannot put us on the front burner if he is embroiled in domestic problems and I don't mean just the normal politics and domestic infighting. What if we start planting the seeds now, that Trump might be a Russian plant, that is a Russian agent doing the bidding of our friend Vladimir?"

Jet's face lit up and he said, "Comrade that is an incredible idea. I can see it now, and it would tie him and his administration up for maybe the entire four years, fighting the democrats, the media and all those that would question his loyalty. What could we call it?" Answering his own question he almost shouted, "Oh, oh, yes, it can be Russian interference, No! Russian collusion. I am on it Comrade."

"Thank you Jet, I thought it might light your fire and of course, I was right as usual. Have a nice trip home and let me hear from you often. You know I always enjoy your thoughtful input."

Jet departed leaving the leader of seven billion people alone with his thoughts as he almost danced his way out to his waiting plane with visions of Russian collusion swirling in his head.

CHAPTER
8

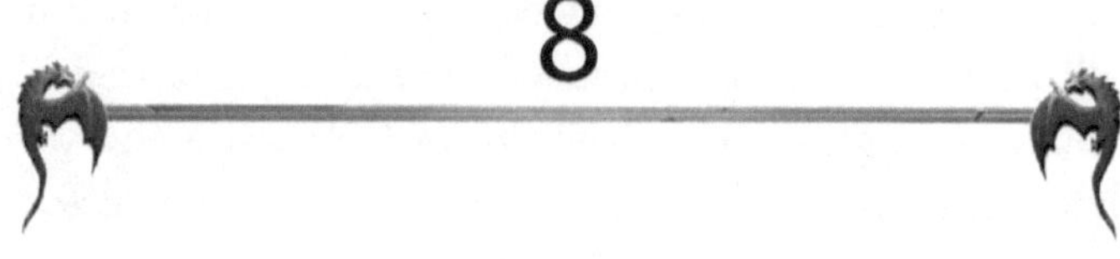

Jet How leaned back in the seat of his luxury jet, as it winged its way from the Chang Chia Tun military complex, and let his mind wander through the door that his President had just opened. It was tantalizing and tempting to rush forward, but he was too astute and too perceptive to rush into anything without going through a complete and detailed logical-thought sequence. He had even designed a form that let him exam almost any problem and sort out the real problem from all the apparent problems.

Throughout the high echelon of the Chinese government he was revered for his thoughtful and sometimes unique solutions. Like his handling of the riots in Tiananmen Square in the spring of 1989, when he was just thirty-five. He put the riots down with an iron hand and his superiors never forgot. It was a defining moment for the regime as protests spread like wildfire across the country. Ben Xiaoping and the other Communist Party leaders deemed the demonstrations to be a serious political threat and gave Jet the authority and three-hundred thousand troops to put an end to the potential regime toppling threat.

Smiling to himself, Jet recalled the fear that tore at him, but fear or no fear, he was up to the job and he did his duty with no thought for the thousands and thousand of lives that were lost in the struggle. It was, he had always told himself, for the Party and he was nothing if he was not a loyal party man.

Nostalgia aside, he cruised and maundered through his filing cabinet brain and early on in the flight had an *ah so* moment. What was his name, what was his name? He could see the face as they had spent several days in London a few years back talking about China and England and how the intelligence agencies of each country could be mutually helpful. Rolling his eyes toward the ceiling, he concentrated and then the light went on; of course, Christopher Sterling. A nice-looking, middle-aged man, with a big head of strawberry blond hair and a jovial smile, who just happened to be one of Britain's top international spies. Sterling knew everything and everybody in the intelligence systems that dotted the planet and Jet even seemed to remember him mentioning that he had been doing major research on Russia and how they tried to influence political outcomes in many countries around the world, including America. Jet judged that Sterling was of the age that he might shortly be retiring and Jet wondered if he would entertain freelance work, but of course he would, big money talked and Jet had big, big money. A smile of sheer sinister calculation crossed Jet's face and he settled deep in his seat, with his eyes closed and started working out a plan of attack.

Reconnecting with the British agent would be easy, but how to approach him with the request that had already been rough-drafted in Jet's mind. After going through all kinds of ways to approach the subject Jet concluded that the direct approach would be best. Just lay out a simple question, indicate that the payday would be substantial, if in fact Christopher could provide incriminating data. Reports, a white paper, a dossier that dug dirt, real or imaginary, on Trump and his business dealings and in Moscow. Yes, that's it, the target had been in Moscow in 2013 promoting a Trump Tower for Moscow. There had to be details that Christopher could get from his Russian agent contacts regarding Trump's dealings in Moscow. He, Trump, might have been on his best behavior but it did not matter as the man had a reputation and rumors were easy to start and easy to perpetuate. If the report was a complete fabrication, so what. The Trump supporters would discount their leaders behavior and the Trump haters would carry the water. Secret negotiations with Vladimir Putin could be included or Trump could promise Putin help and cover if he ever did become President which several years ago would, of course, have been outside the bounds of possibility. Thinking out loud Jet concluded, mouthing the words quietly, "I'll just tell Christopher I want all the dirt he can dig, from

Russian agents, or any other source, on Trump, Russia and Trump's relationship with Putin."

Opening his eyes and returning to the luxury of his surroundings, Jet glanced out the window and saw that the smog of Beijing was on the horizon. It was an axiomatic fact that China and the Green Peace star-gazers of the world could not acknowledge, but he was beginning to smell it and his eyes were smarting so it was, of course, true; regardless of what the Climate Change people preached. Jet knew for a fact that there were over one thousand coal fired generating plants, belching out smoke twenty-four/seven and that 121 gigawatts of coal plants were under construction, which is more than the rest of the world combined. He just shook his head and wondered if the stupid tree huggers would ever face reality.

Packing up his briefcase, preparing to deplane, he found himself looking forward to an evening with his wife's sister, an arrangement that had been going on for the past two years and one he still could not understand. He smiled to himself and thought, 'You can be the smartest man in China and still not understand women.'

CHAPTER
9

n his private and very secure ground floor office, in a government complex, on the outskirts of Beijing, Jet How Chung had spent all morning planning his campaign against Donald J. Trump.

First on his agenda had been a call to the Chinese ambassador in London, no matter that it was 2 a.m. London time, to inform him that it was urgent that the Ambassador locate Christopher Sterling and arrange a meeting for Jet and the British spy. The ambassador was not privileged as to the reason for the meeting, but knew that the President's point-man requests took top priority and the ambassador gushed that he would track down the agent and set up a meeting just as soon as possible. He ended his groveling response by asking, "Comrade will you come to London for the meeting?"

"Yes, Comrade ambassador, I shall be on my way the minute you have a confirmed schedule with Mr. Sterling."

Jet pushed the disconnect button, looked at his Rolex and knew that in a few minutes the Director of University Programs for North America would be arriving. He had developed a list of organizations he wanted the university director to court, integrate into his operational base, and to fund. The list contained the names of the top dissenting groups in America and he knew that they all had common goals. They all hated Republicans, free enterprise and capitalism, and his gut told him that soon their list of dislikes would be headed by one Donald J. Trump.

Target List

Occupy, Black Lives Matter, Our Revolution, Sister District Project, Knock Every Door, Swing Left, Flippable, Resurgent Left, Adopt-a-State, Open 45, Movement 2015, The Pussyhat Project, Global Justice Movement, Friends of Abe.

Looking over the list, he was amazed that he had not heard or read about most of these technocrat groups, while others seemed to be in the news on a daily basis. The 'Occupy' movement that had started with discontents occupying New York's Zuccotti Park, in September of 2011, seemed to be the best known. Their sociopolitical movement expressed opposition to social and economic inequality and to the lack of real democracy around the world. By October of 2011, the Occupy protests had taken root in 82 countries and over 950 cities around the world. In America over 600 cities had experienced their social eruptions. Jet had noticed that the political candidates from the left (Bernie Sanders and Hillary Clinton) had picked up on the seeds of discourse that Occupy sowed and even Republicans like Jeb Bush, Ted Cruz and Marco Rubio could be found mouthing and supporting some of the ideas that Occupy brought to the table.

A series of chime sounds interrupted Jet's thoughts and he pushed the intercom button and asked, "Is Lin Lee here?"

The voice from the outside waiting room confirmed his question and as Jet rose to cross the room, to the door that Lin Lee would enter, he said, "Send him in."

Lin Lee was a trim, athletic type that bound through the door with his ever present smile, welcoming the chance to be in the presence of one of the countries top leaders. "Comrade Chung, so good to see you again. Life must be agreeing with you as you look younger than when we last met."

Jet smiled the, 'I have been there, heard that before' smile and shook the young man's hand, indicated he should be seated in one of the elegant side chairs, that ringed Jet's desk. Before Lin could say anything, Jet spoke. "I suppose you are wondering why I sent for you on such short notice?"

"Yes, Comrade."

"Well, I have a new assignment for you that is extremely important to the well being of our party and the country. This project is so critical that there will be no written instructions and should anyone question the work you will be doing, all you have to say is, 'I am proceeding at the direction of Comrade President.' If that does not solve the inquiry or questions and the party asking seems overly concerned and becomes intrusive, inform them that they can check with me and I will straighten them out. Understood?"

"Yes, Comrade and thank you for allowing me to bear this responsibility, whatever it may be."

Jet cocked his head and smiled at the young man and continued, "Lin you will have a budget of thirty million US dollars," Lin's mouth dropped and he actually felt light-headed, his mind raced ahead, 'they are entrusting me with thirty million dollars, me, Lin Lee?' "And today I will open that account with The People's Bank of China and your contact there will be the second in command Xi Jinping. You will use the money to help fund these fourteen groups," Jet handed Lin a one-page document listing the groups, "And in return I hope that the leadership of each group will welcome your student-agents into their organizations not only as workers but in leadership positions. Are you following me son?"

"Yes, yes, of course Comrade. You want me to use the student-agents we have in almost every American university and college to infiltrate these organizations, but for what purpose?"

Jet leaned back in his chair, stared at the ornate two-story roof of his office, with ceiling fans slowly turning and did not reply for almost three minutes, which to Lin seemed like the longest wait of his life. 'Had he gone too far? Jumping the gun without waiting for Jet to explain. His ancestors were turning over in their graves, he was sure.'

"Lin, I, we want to make a dramatic and lasting impact on the upcoming American elections. We think that the Republican candidate could well be Donald Trump and if that comes to pass we want to do all in our power to prevent his election. That is the real reason, but that is not to be shared outside this room. Understood'?"

"Yes, Comrade, fully understood."

"The apparent reason, that you will explain to all that need to know, is that the Chinese students, studying in America, are brothers and sisters of the sociopolitical movements and they wish to support these groups with active participation so they can grow and learn from the experience. Please repeat back what I have just told you, in your own words, as if you were explaining the program to one of your student-agents; outlining what you want them to accomplish,"

Lin Lee, sat looking at Jet, reaching deep within his brain, knowing that the next few minutes would define his life and career as well as the lives of his extended family. 'A mistake and you and all you love can disappear, with absolutely no trace. No trace that you ever walked the world, ever loved, ever savored a sunrise. Absolutely no trace, no trace, no trace.' 'Sweat beads popped up on his forehead that did not go unnoticed by the master manipulator.'

Slowly Lin started his reply, "Chinese student X, we, the Chinese government and the Chinese Communist Party deeply appreciate the work that you have been doing during your stay in America. It is important work that will be richly rewarded once you complete your studies and return to the motherland, which I know is your primary goal. We have a new program that we wish you to help us implement and we have selected you to lead this important work with the local chapter of Occupy Wall Street. We want you to become active in all their projects and we want you to make them understand that you not only want to donate your time and energy but your family fortune as well and that you will bring all your friends and associates, from the Chinese community, to help. You are so committed to their social and economic agenda, and for that matter all Global Justice matters, and you want to work tirelessly to help them realize their goals and aspirations. Questions?"

Lin looked at Jet and the normal penetrating black eyes that could cut you to ribbons were soft and absorbent. "Well Lin, I made yet another historical choice when I chose you to lead this program. You understand from your toes up what I am looking for and I know that you and your charges will rise to the level that the President and I require. Tell me how many cells do you currently have working the American colleges and universities?"

"Just a few over three-thousand. The smallest unit may have ten members and the largest unit is well over one-hundred, with the average probably being near thirty members per campus. We also have faculty and staff members in key university positions like Yanqing Ye at Boston University, Zaosong Zheng at Beth Israel Medical center and even some American professors that are actively working for our cause; for money of course. As you know last year we had over 280,000 students in our USA Thousand Talents Plan and we projected that number will increase to over 350,000 by 2018. Of course only the best and brightest are worked into what we call 'agent' level and they are given specific assignments with regard to the information pipeline that we want them to establish and keep full." Smiling Lin added, "I tell them it's like a brewery. If you want good beer coming out every day in abundant quantities you must keep the vats full of wheat, barley, malt, hops and clean clear water. If the student wants to finish his or her education, climb the party ladder and become a leader, they must keep the pipeline full, and that requires daily effort. The sheer volume of data being funneled into our system in is almost mindboggling. The work requires over a hundred thousand technicians to sort, catalog and see that the raw data gets directed to the appropriate industries. Most of the data is cutting edge technology and having the experts to sift and sort and assimilate the data is an incredibly important part of the program." Lin caught himself and said meekly, "I'm sorry. Don't know why I thought I had to explain the system to the creator. Sorry Comrade."

Jet smiled his really evil smile and said, "No problem Lin. I like to see you excited about your work. Makes me know that my selection process was 'spot-on' as the British like to say."

"Thank you Comrade Chung for your understanding."

"Let's see, 30 million divided by 3000 equals about 10,000 US dollars and therefore we have established your funding parameters for each of the university groups you will be directing, however you may need more or less, depending on the unique aspects of each group but you will, I'm sure, develop a system that will make the maximum use of the money allocated. I would hope that you will give weight to the funding levels based on the location. By that, I mean in those blue states where a Republican candidate has no chance, like California, you may go light whereas in the red states, where it will be a dog fight, you may wish to go heavy. Remember, in America it is not the popular vote that determines the winner. Hillary could well win the popular vote but if she does not win the swing states, then she will lose. The primary swing states will most likely be Colorado, Florida, Iowa, Michigan, Minnesota, Nevada, New Hampshire, North Carolina, Ohio, Pennsylvania and Virginia. But there is a sub-list that is critical as well like Arizona, Georgia, New Mexico, Oregon and Wisconsin. As noted, you will need to spend most of your money in the swing states, so even though it is a Herculean task, to make the right selections, you at least have a starting point. Agreed?"

"Yes, Jet I understand and will I be required to get detailed approval once I have each specific plan worked out?"

"No. Delegation is authority with responsibility. It is a process of entrusting responsibilities and authorities to others with the establishment of complete accountability. Therefore, delegation is the forcing downward, in the structure of organization, responsibilities with commensurate authorities. Lin, you have the responsibility, you have the authority and we, the President and I, have confidence that you will always make decisions and do what is best for the party and the country." With eyes flashing Jet continued, "We trust your judgment and we know you will not abuse that trust nor will we micro-manage from afar. You will be on the front line, you will be ram-rodding the program and we are counting on you to be successful."

The implications were not wasted on Lin Lee. He knew instinctively that he was being given the rope. It could hang him or help pull him to the top. The choice was his.

CHAPTER
10

Lin Lee had not been gone ten minutes when Jet's phone rang and removing it from the charging platform, he started the call like he started every call, "Jet here."

The voice on the other end identified himself as the English Ambassador and proceeded to update Jet, advising him that Christopher Sterling was currently out of country, but that he had been able to confirm a meeting with Jet, at the London Embassy, on August 5th or 6th, if that was acceptable. "Yes, Comrade that is acceptable. I will arrive in London on the 4th, please make all the appropriate arrangements and thank you for your help."

In London the Ambassador's body gave an involuntary overall spine-chilling shake as the line clicked dead. The Ambassador shook his head to clear the image of himself in front of a firing squad and said under his breath, "That man will be the death of me and all my line. Careful, careful, careful."

Jet was certain that the Ambassador was still shaking from the crisp exchange and Jet loved the power he meted out so well. He knew the Ambassador would be on pins and needles for the next thirty some days, in anticipation of Jet's arrival, and that is the way he like to operate. He could read people so much better when they were scared, and fear and terror had been his modus operandi since the Tiananmen Square days.

Leaving his desk and moving to the other side of the room, he sat down on a big red leather couch, flipped on the TV and tuned in FOX News to get the latest take on the upcoming Republican debates that would go down just about the time he was in London. Jet noted, that as usual, Trump was the main news lead and he carefully concluded that none of the other candidates were doing or said anything to excite their base. Jet was amazed that all the pundits praised the only woman in the race, Carly Fiorina, and had little to say about Trump, other than he might be a third-party candidate if things did not go his way. All the negative talk about Trump did not sway Jet in the least, he still had the gut feeling that Trump would street fight his way into the catbird seat and that all the plans and the Zhanlue's being developed would help turn the tide and get Hillary elected. That he knew would ensure China of eight more years of American indifference. Smiling to himself Jet thought, 'God's of my ancestors just give us eight more years and we will bury America. They won't know what happened and when they finally wake up, if they ever do, it will be too late. China will be the world leader, i.e. master.'

Looking back on this fading day, Jet could not help but be pleased with the outcome of his plans. Lin Lee was going to be successful and he was sure that the meeting with Christopher Sterling would be a world changer. It really was simple; dig dirt, true or false, spread it around and let Trump try to prove his innocence. The whole matter could very well distract him for the full four years, if the flukes of flukes happened and he managed to beat Hillary. On the other hand, Hillary would be like putty in their hands, as had been Bill. She would undoubtedly continue the Obama "Don't look and you won't see" programs that had let China rise from a second tier player to the largest economy in the world by 2014. Jet chuckled out loud, knowing that current projections showed that China's factory output would be as much as the sum of the US, Japan and Europe in just ten short years.

Sinking deeper into the couch he put his head back, closed his eyes and remembered Obama's first visit to China in 2009. How could he forget, as it was an unbelievable moment, etched in his brain forever. Jet remembered confronting the new president, on Air Force One with documentation that proved beyond a shadow of a doubt that Mr. Obama was born in Kenya and not Hawaii, as he had always claimed. China never had to go public as almost every China request was met with approval by the leader of the free world. The papers were still in Jet's safe and would never be made public during Barack Obama's lifetime. Jet had promised and he prided himself on his word being his bond.

CHAPTER
11

J et How Chung sat alone in the Ambassador's private office on August 6, 2015 waiting for the arrival of Christopher Sterling. Jet had no notes, but then he seldom used notes as he had a brain that seemed to thrive on detail and order. A soft knock on the door announced Agent Sterling's arrival and Jet rose to greet his visitor, who was exactly as Jet had remembered. Sort of chunky for his height, big head of hair, a pleasant smile and an ornate walking stick that he treated like a third arm. Rumor had it that the walking stick had belonged to Winston Churchill.

As the two men shook hands and gravitated toward two elegant side chairs from the Yang Dynasty (1271-1368), that were placed in front of a shuttered fireplace, Jet's guest started the dialog by saying, "I was intrigued when I heard from the Ambassador that you wanted to meet with me and since then I have been walking different scenarios around my head and to tell you the truth I have no clue as to why you requested this meeting, and I can't wait to find out."

Jet gave his visitor an admiring look and replied, "Well, Christopher a special project recently came across my desk and the minute I read the requirements your smiling face popped into my old brain. The requirements call for quick, intelligent and highly confidential information and I could think of no one that could do a better job of collecting the needed data than yourself."

"And Mr. China, as some of my associates call you, what would you like me to collect?"

Jet looked across the space separating the two men and replied in a low voice, "I would like you to collect information on a United States citizen. Your fee will be ten million U.S. dollars, half paid today and the balance paid upon completion of your research and the publication of that research by an American media outlet of your choice."

Jet reached inside his jacket breast pocket, removed a blank envelope and handed it to Christopher Sterling without a word. The British agent opened the unsealed envelop and his eyes got as big as saucers as he fingered a cashier's check for five million dollars, drawn on the Chase Manhattan Bank, with the maker shown as Fussion GPS. After going over every detail of the check, Christopher looked at the Chinese gentleman seated across from him and commented, "Well, Jet this certainly looks like a untraceable document."

Jet smiled and replied, "Yes, it is and I am certain that your Banker in Zurich will have no trouble verifying the authenticity and adding the proceeds to your account."

"Jet, what and who is Fussion GPS?"

"It is an American think-tank company that helps clients with a full range of political problems and the two principals that started the organization received their initial underwriting from yours truly; of course, that information is not trackable as well." "So, there is no way that anyone will ever know that you are the driving force behind this organization and that we have ever done business."

"Of course, Christopher and I am pleased you were able to come to that conclusion so quickly, as it saves much discussion and foot dancing, if you know what I mean?"

"Yes, Jet I know what you mean and I will proceed with the rest of my life, knowing that this meeting never happened. Can you give me parameters as to what kind of report you wish me to generate?"

"Of course. I want you to collect and publish as much dirt as you can find on the subject. He has international playboy status and I want all the seamy details of his past life exposed. Nothing is too sensitive and nothing should be excluded, let it all out. And, Christopher, if you need bribe money let me know the amounts and it will be added to your final check. Understand?"

"Yes, but what if my contacts are unable to come up with any meaningful dirt, what if we just can't find any reliable sources. How will that impact the final payment if we are unable to deliver what you want."

"Christopher, we want you to find and expose dirt and if you are unable to locate credible and believable witnesses then manufacture them, as you see fit. Your report is meant to do one thing and one thing only and I do not care where the data comes from; however, you may want to start with your contacts in Russia and Ukraine. Just take the inquiry wherever it leads you. I only care that it fulfills the requirements of destroying the reputation of Donald J. Trump and if need be his family."

"I don't understand how China can possibly conceive Trump to be a ten million dollar threat; after all he is just one of a dozen or more that are running and from what I read his chances are nil to none?"

"Yes, that may be true Christopher but we are looking at it as insurance. You are providing us with an insurance policy, no more, no less. So Christopher are you in the insurance business?"

Christopher Sterling returned the check to the envelope and deposited it in his breast coat pocket. Standing up he said, "It has been nice seeing you again and I trust that in a few months you will find my work acceptable."

"I shall look forward to seeing your report and thank you again for coming on such short notice." As if an afterthought had suddenly came over Jet, he asked, "Will you please follow me as we would like your exit from the embassy to go unrecorded by the spies across the street?"

Christopher acknowledged Jet's instructions with a thumbs up and followed him through a series of passageways that exited into the rear of a bookstore located on the opposite side of the block.

"Thank you again for coming and I shall anxiously await your report."

Christopher Sterling nodded and made his way from the back of the building, through the musty, dusty shelves and exited the store front into the noisy London world.

He quickly hailed a cab and said to the hackney, "Credit Suisse Bank, number one Cabot Square, and driver, ten pounds extra if you get me there before noon."

Leaning back he closed his eyes, let his left hand confirm that the envelope was firmly deposited in his breast coat pocket and visualized himself on his new yacht, cruising the warm blue Mediterranean waters with a group of admiring young ladies, clad in the skimpy bikinis, all at his beckon call.

Jet returned to the ambassador's office, which had been reoccupied by the ambassador and said in an all-business voice. "Please have a driver ready within the hour. I will be going to Heathrow for the flight home. Thank you again for your hospitality and I shall be certain to give the President your fondest greetings."

The ambassador gushed his appreciation as Jet departed for the water closet.

CHAPTER
12

The August 30 meeting of the group of five followed the same format as all the previous meetings and at the same venue. President Hu was in rare form and Jet was pleased to see him so upbeat and positive about almost everything. The Rainbow Zhanlue had worked and worked beyond their wildest dreams. China was leading the world charge and the new ten-year projections showed that their factory output would, within ten years, surpass that of Japan, Europe and the USA combined. The President of the People's Republic of China was almost euphoric and his greetings were sincere and thoughtful and made each member feel like a cloud walking god.

"Well Comrades, the ancestors are shining on our individual and collective efforts and I look forward to hearing more good news from each of you. Let's start with Comrade Jet."

Jet rose and acknowledged each smiling face, thanked his leader and opened his remarks with, "Comrades, I have concluded important arrangements with overseas associates and my campaign to deny Mr. Trump his aspirations is well underway. You may have noted from recent news reports that he is drawing big crowds, but the political pundits don't think he has staying power and that eventually he will put his large foot in his even larger mouth." Jet waited for the chuckles to subside and then continued, "The first debates, earlier this month, were not positive for him and even though I still think he is the dark horse, I am not as worried as when he first announced his candidacy. We are in the process of joining the major protest groups in America, through our university action groups and we will look for these groups to move Trump to the top of their hate list, at least that will be our goal."

"Thank you for your attention and if anyone has any questions please make your concerns known." Jet re-seated himself as no one jumped into the arena.

President Hu asked, "Questions anyone? Well if not I have just one Jet and that is, who do you now think will be the Republican candidate?"

Jet smiled at his leader and said, "I still have my money on Trump, but I hope I am wrong."

"Lin, can you give us an update on your efforts to control the world market on pharmaceutical and health related supplies?"

"Certainly Comrade President." as he stood and surveyed his fellow travelers and started, "As I reported last time our goal is to capture the American, and world, health care supply markets. We now have hundreds of Chinese company executives traveling the world and each success they achieve adds to our percentage of market. We had to establish a clearing house at my headquarters in the capital and there are now over 4,000 people cataloging and compelling the data. We will shortly be issuing a report that shows our percentage of world market share one year ago and our projected market shares by the end of this year. I think the results will be dramatic, but we now think that the growth in 2017 and 18 will even be more spectacular as new plants and facilities come on line. So far, we have not had to use a fraction of the budget that was established for this project, but that may spike up in the next few months as we continue down the road. Questions?"

President Hu commented that he would look forward to the market share data and thanked the minister for his input.

"Well General how are you coming on nation building?"

"Wish I had some dramatic news but this is basically a training and educational program for the Army brass and there is no practical way to judge how effective our the training is being received by the troops. We, of course, demand rigid classroom participation and have established tests, to judge proficiency, but without actual boots on the ground, at some foreign location, it is difficult to judge the results of our efforts. If anyone has any suggestions, I would be eager to hear your input."

Looking around the room for help the General found Jet looking thoughtful and asked, "Comrade Jet do you have any suggestions?"

"Yes, yes I do comrade. Would it be possible to take one of our cities, located in the western deserts and use it as a test facility? By that I mean you could pretend it was a foreign capital and that it was on its knees because of the economic policies we forced on the country. You could then have hands on training for the troops, as to how they would take over and run the local government. All the utilities could be commandeered by the Army and the troops could learn how to deliver the service to keep the local population alive and under their thumb. Just a thought Comrade."

President Hu jumped in and asked, "Would that help you General?"

"Yes, I believe it would. There is nothing like combat to train a soldier and this would be as close to combat as we could come. Do I have your approval to research and come up with a plan for a specific area?"

Before the President could reply Jet said, with his evil smile in full view, "Maybe there is a city in Tibet that might fit the bill."

President Hu looked at his friend and asked, "Does that mind of your ever shut down?"

Jet just smiled and under his breath said, "Only when I'm with the opposite sex comrade."

The room erupted in laughter and when President Hu had dabbed his eyes with his ever-present white handkerchief, he thanked the General and Jet for their input and finished by saying, "I will look forward to your next report General."

"Yes, Sir!" was the terse reply.

"Well Admiral it's down to you. What can you tell us?"

"Comrades our research to date suggests that unless we find new protein sources that the hunger problem, on planet earth, will be acute in just thirty years. By 2050 the United Nations has projected that the earth's population will be almost 9 billion, verses today's 7.3 billion and that will put pressure on all areas of agriculture. By 2075 population will peak at 9.22 billion and will then start to decline. The decline will come as fertility rates fall below replacement levels. By 2050 Europe will hit its low point in growth and Africa will not get to its low level until 2130. Europe's share of world population will be cut from about 12 percent to 5 percent and during this same period Africa's share will double from 13 percent to almost 25 percent. In Asia population rates will increase in the west and decline in the east and Asia, instead of being four-and-a half times as populous as Africa, will only be 2.2 times as populous. So you can see big changes are coming for most of the world but for North America things will stay relative static and that is because of the immigration magnet that it represents. Fertility rates will decline like the rest of the world, but immigration will be strong and therefore North America will neither make great gains or losses." Pausing the Admiral continued, "On the food front we are looking at every fishery in the world, at all marginal lands and will soon have firm recommendations for getting us through the population changes that will be coming. Questions?"

President Hu interjected, "Looks like we will need to put more effort into projecting our presence in Africa. Thank you Admiral for a thought-provoking report."

Looking around the room the President continued, "I can report that the Chaoxue lab is up and running and we are starting to transfer the work we have been doing in Wuhan to the new facility. We will only transfer the highly classified research so that the world will assume that WUHAN is our primary research center. So far we have encountered no problems with the physical plant and the people are beginning to lock into their new responsibilities and duties. I will not mention the lab again, until I have news on some of the products they are developing. This meeting stands adjourned and I will look forward to seeing you all back here in mid-December. Thank you again for your participation. Jet, may I see you in my office please?"

President Hu and Jet watched the others file out and then moved from the conference room to the President's next door office and the comfortable couch by the fireplace. The President opened with a frank question. "I was wondering Comrade is there any way your dealings with the British agent can be traced back to our doorstep?"

"Not to worry Yanlin, I have covered the trail deep and I have a plan for later on that will make it appear that the Democratic party was the funding source for the report or dossier."

"Good, I knew you would cover the tracks, but we can't be to careful. Do you really think Mr. Trump has a chance?"

"Yes, right now it is slim, but the masses seem to like his tough talk and style and I just have that deep gut feeling that he will pull it off."

"Jet, what are your overall plans for the rest of the year?"

"Trump is job one, but I have some interesting irons in the fire and I look forward to sharing them with you as the details come together and they move from the theoretical into the realm of possibility."

"I'll be flying home tomorrow, could we share dinner tonight or do you have other, more enjoyable plans?"

"Dinner will be fine; on the outdoor patio around seven."

Jet pulled himself up off the couch and left the President with his thoughts after saying with his big smile, "I won't be late."

CHAPTER
13

After Jet departed, the President sat quietly for several minutes and then reluctantly reached inside his coat pocket and removed a sealed envelope that he had received right before the Group 5 meeting. The communication was from the Chaoxue lab director and had been delivered by military courier indicating that the documents were highly classified. With heavy apprehension the president broke the seal and removed the two-page document, written by the Director Yang.

' My President,

It is with a heavy hand that I write you about recent developments that have come to my attention. As you know we are in the process of moving highly classified research projects from the Wuhan Lab to our new facility, and during the transfer I have discovered a complete breakdown in security by the Wuhan Lab director and his key subordinates. They have been secretive about their work and have actually tried to hide sensitive projects that they deem too important to transfer to the new Chaoxue lab. Doctors Xi, Wong, and Youxia are the responsible parties and I think that their lab assistants and secretaries are suspect as well. We have also noted breaches of protocol under their leadership that could possibly facilitate the release of a killer virus into the Wuhan city population and possibly beyond. My security team has seized control of the Wuhan facility and the above named personnel and their key employees are being held under arrest at the facility. One stunning concern is that they have been doing research on wild animals, such as bats and snakes and then selling the carcasses to the local wet meat markets to earn extra income. We have no way to know if this practice resulted in tainted meat being supplied to the local market. Comrade President, I chose not to go up my chain of command but rather come directly to you, considering the sensitive nature of the Chaoxue lab and the mission that you personally entrusted to me and my staff.

I await you instructions Comrade President.

Dr. Lin Kit Yang'

President Hu sunk deeper in the leather couch, put his head back, closed his eyes and let the information he had just received bounce off every corner of his brain. After almost an hour of consideration he opened up his cellphone and dialed Jet's number.

"Jet How here. How can I serve you Yanlin?"

"Jet, please come back to the office. I need your help."

"I will be there in a few minutes Yanlin."

As good as his word the office door opened almost before the President had set down the phone and Jet's smiling face appeared around the door. "How can I be of service Comrade?"

The President handed Jet the letter and seemed to sink deeper into the couch. Jet sat down in one of the side chairs and slowly read the two-page letter. When he finished, he looked at the President Zent and asked, "Do you want me to go to Wuhan and handle this matter?"

President Hu nodded yes, and then leaned his head back on the couch and closed his eyes. Jet waited several minutes, replaced the letter in the envelope, laid the envelope on the couch next to the President and exited the office. Within minutes Jet's staff were in the process of readying his plane for the flight to Wuhan and the Director of the Chaoxue lab was notified, by highly classified e-mail that Jet was on the way and would meet the director at the Wuhan Air Base by 1900 hours. The last paragraph of the e-mail requested the Director to have his security forces round up all family members of the three doctors, their assistants and secretaries and take them to the Wuhan Air Base which was part of the Guangzhou Military Region. Another secure communication directed to the Commanding General of the Wuhan Air Base notified him of Jets impending arrival and that Dr. Lin Kit Yang would be arriving at the air base with his security forces and a group of detainees and that the Doctor was to be given any assistance he might require.

Before Jet's plane lifted off a handwritten note had been delivered to the President's office that read, 'Sorry to miss dinner, I shall report tomorrow on outcome of Wuhan trip Jet.' During the two-hour flight the Commanding General of the Guangazhou Military Region was advised that the President's point man was on the way to the Wuhan Air base and that prompted a scramble of major proportions. The General himself commanded a flight of J-31 fighter jets (Jianjiji-31) that arrived at the Wuhan air base fifteen minutes before Jet's plane swooped in for a hot landing at the remote base.

As Jet deplaned the General stepped forward and welcomed his elite visitor, with the base commander and more brass bringing up the rear. "Thank you General for meeting me. Is there an auditorium where we can meet? I think our Dr. Yang will be here shortly with about 150 people so we need to accommodate that number." "Yes, Comrade we have a secure hanger that will fill you needs and I have just been advised that Dr. Yang and his security force are currently at the front gate. I will have them directed to the hangar. Is there anything else you require?"

"No, other than the doctor and his charges and me and my staff will be the only people in the hangar and a high security status will be in place around the facility. Understood?"

"Of course Comrade. It will be as you say."

"And General on the most remote part of this base I want a pit dug that can accommodate 150 bodies and Sir, that needs to be done within the next hour." The piercing eyes that instructed the General left no doubt in the General's mind that this was indeed the man that had put down the Tiananmen Square riots. There was no remorse, no sense of moral outrage, just cold, hard reality. The General turned on his heels and huddled with junior officers who went scurrying into the twilight on their specific missions.

"Shall we go to the hangar General?"

"Of course comrade, the car is right over here."

Jet and the General rode in the first staff car and Jet's staff followed in two more. The ride to the hangar was short and as they pulled up to the building, three busses from the Wuhan transit system were parked near the hanger entrance and Dr Yang and the Base Commander were the only people outside the busses, other than the security detail that the doctor had brought with him.

Jet exited the staff car and walked over to the doctor, put his arm around his shoulder and walked off a few paces where they could speak in private. "Doctor I am sorry we have to meet again under such difficult circumstances."

" I too, Comrade."

"I read your report to the President and I think we have to take this as a serious and unforgivable breach of trust and that these treasonous actions must be punished. Tell me how many people are in the buses?"

"There are 134 Comrade. The three doctors, their nine assistants and three clerks and those fifteen peoples extended families which amounts to 119 men, women and children. We have not collected mothers, fathers or aunts and uncles of the fifteen principals which we judge would be another fifty or so."

Jet considered what he had just heard and staring right through the doctor, or so it seemed to Dr Yang, announced slowly, "I think what you have here makes a big enough statement. You and your staff and security agents may return to the lab and continue with your transfer work. Turning toward the base commander Jet ordered, "General, see that Dr. Yang and his staff and security agents are returned to the Wuhan Lab."

"Yes, Sir, right away Sir. Doctor please follow me,"

Doctor Yang, his five assistants and the fifteen-man security force followed the General away from the buses and toward the base headquarters, where a line of staff cars were parked. As they loaded up and departed toward the air base gate each person knew that those left on the buses were no longer of this earth and they also knew that it could happen to them just as fast and just as quick. There was no talk, no noise of any kind as the survivors rode back toward life and their duty to the state.

Jet turned to the officer at his side and said, "Instead of off loading the detainees, into the hangar, I now prefer to speak to each bus; please provide me with an armed security officer."

The General patted his hip and said, "Will I do?"

"Yes, let's get on with it," Jet said as they headed for the first bus. The bus driver was standing by his vehicle and opened the doors as Jet and the military officer arrived. "General, will you please replace the driver and the other two with military police officers and have a car take them back to town."

"Yes, Sir."

Jet went up the steps of the bus, with the General right behind him and immediately quiet greeted him. He asked in a calm voice, "Are doctors Wong, Xi or Youxia on this bus."

From near the front a voice said, "I am Doctor Wong. The other two doctors are on the other busses."

"Dr. Wong, you have committed unpardonable crimes against your country and your fellow countrymen. There is no place in this society for such treason, which does not have to be proved in a court, because I ask you here and now to admit your crimes, which could have put the whole country, for that fact the whole world's populations at risk. Do you so specify?"

"Yes, I did what you say but can you please spare my family and coworkers as they had no knowledge or part in my transgressions?"

"Your request is denied."

With that Jet turned and followed the General to the second bus and then the third, and in each case the message was the same.

At the conclusion Jet turned to the Commander and ask, "Has the digging been completed?"

"Yes, Comrade."

"Then form up an execution squad and put these people in their final resting place and return the land to its original state with no indication or marker. Questions?"

Shaking, the General humbly ask, "Do I need signed orders Sir?" If looks could kill the General was dead, but Jet just replied in a calm and cool voice, "General, I am acting on direct orders from the Supreme Commander and President of this country. Carry out your orders or join those on the bus." The evil smile that accompanied the words made the General's heart almost stop.

Jet turned on his heels and walked quickly toward his staff that had been waiting and watching his every move. Approaching the group, Jet said to the base commander, "Please arrange for our transportation back to my plane and notify the tower we will be departing shortly."

Heels clicked, sharp commands were given and Jet and his staff were whisk away to the flight line where the private jet was waiting.

Once air borne Jet e-mailed his leader a short message that read, 'Mission accomplished. Heading home. See you soon. Dr. Yang will need a new director and staff for Wuhan Lab.'

The Wuhan trip had taken a toll on Jet like nothing he had ever experienced. Six days later he was still wrestling with his decision, and he found himself drinking more than usual and staying up late. On the night of September fifth, he was setting on his patio, overlooking Beijing, and glancing at his watch and noted that it was only an hour away from midnight, time for bed, and another restless night. Suddenly off to the east the sky blazed up and within minutes a shock wave rattled past. He immediately picked up the phone, dialed the duty officer at his office in Beijing and ask, "Do you know anything about an explosion in the Tianjin area?" The officer indicated he did not but would check and get back to his superior as soon as he could come up with any information.

The lights on the horizon fluttered and then faded away and then a second and more powerful explosion illuminated the landscape for the second time in minutes. Jet's brain went into overdrive and latched onto a piece of information from the past, so he immediately knew, without a doubt, that the hazardous chemical facility at the port of Tainjin must have suffered a horrendous accident. The duty office called within minutes and confirmed that Jet's suspicion was correct.

The carnage went on over four days and when it was finally under control 104 firemen had lost their lives and 77 civilians were dead or missing. When the reports finally surfaced, they showed that over 880 tons of ammonium nitrate (equivalent to 336 tons of TNT) had wiped out the port area and much of the surrounding business and housing areas. Thousands were displaced and it would take over two years for the port to return to some degree of normalcy.

Since sleep didn't seem to be on the menu so Jet flipped on the TV and dialed in FOX news, from Washington, to see what the political landscape was looking like in America. It was 11 a.m. in Washington D.C. and Howard Kurtz, one of the FOX hosts was saying, "Virtually all the political prognosticators are united on one point: Donald Trump's surge is fascinating, but of course he won't be the Republican nominee."

Well, thought Jet, 'Maybe I don't have to worry or be concerned after all, Mr. Kurtz usually knows what the hell he is talking about.' Then smiling to himself, he repeated the word, 'usually' and then continued, 'but I'm sorry Howard my money is still on Mr. Trump and if you were any kind of real reporter you would move past the Washington suburbs and find out what the Americans in Nebraska and Michigan are thinking.'

The good looking hostess, one of the FOX info babes, launched into the Republican debate schedule and Jet noted that through the end of the year there would be one debate per month but then the pace picked up with two in January, three in February and two in March. She, too, gushed on and on that Trump could not possibly win and that the convention in mid-July would be for Bush or Cruz to lose.

Jet made a mental note to check in with Lin Lee and see how he was doing on his project to infiltrate the American protest groups, but maybe the boy needed more time, after all not everyone in the loop had the "Jet" work ethic. Finally feeling tired and out of sorts Jet retired and noted as he took to his bed that it was already 2 a.m. and he had important meetings in just seven hours.

CHAPTER
15

The last quarter of 2015 was a time of reflection for Jet and President Hu as they met often and wrestled with the problems of the world and the blooming of China. President Hu noticed that his old friend was different, more reflective, more shades of gray than the black and white man that he had been since his rise to national prominence.

They spent hours, days and weeks talking, plotting and reviewing their place in the three thousand years of Chinese recorded history, starting with the Shang Dynasty (1600-1046 BC).

Between 1978 and 2005 the Chinese economy, under President Hu's guidance, had grown almost ten percent cent per year. The growth had transformed China from a state dominated socialist economy to a mixed economy. Accompanying the growth were high levels of industrialization and urbanization which influenced every aspect of China's societal, cultural and economic fabric.

Just this year President Hu had initiated the "Made in China 2025" plan which would upgrade and modernize China's manufacturing in ten key sectors through extensive governmental assistance. China's growth was tied to the America wagon in that trade between the two countries grew from $5 billion in 1980 to almost $500 billion by 2015.

In addition, China launched a massive program to purchase U. S. Treasury securities and their projected purchases totaled well over one trillion dollars. The Chinese President called the purchase plan The Rainbow Zhanlue (Strategy) and during the Obama years it was this proven policy that allowed China to reach their goal of surpassing the USA economy. The treasury bond purchases enabled the U.S. government to keep interest rates relatively low and at the same time helped China remain competitive so it seemed to be a win-win for both sides. At least that is how Presidents Obama and Bush and Clinton chose to think about the relationship, when they were counting their China based fortunes.

It was already Friday November 20 and in just a little over a week the Chinese leader would be addressing the Paris United National Climate Change Summit, never mind that China was one of the worst polluters on the planet. The climate change zealots at the United Nations chose to ignore the facts because China mouthed the words and made grandiose promises they wanted to hear, none of which would ever come to pass.

Getting ready for summit President Hu had been reviewing various reports from around the world and one such was the July 2014 report by Lisa Williams of the Lowy Institute, an international think-tank based in Australia. Looking over his glasses at Jet How who was wedged into the couch that fronted the fireplace he asked, "Jet did you read the report that the Lowy group, of Australia, wrote about our energy policies?"

Jet thought for a minute and then replied, "Yes Yanlin I recall that it was not too complementary but I think it was accurate at least from what I remember. Why?"

Listen to this, as the President started reading from the report, "China's carbon dioxide emissions dwarf the contributions of all other nations, at more than a quarter of the world total. The countries' emissions are already more than 20 times greater than Australia's and if current policies remain unchanged, by 2020 China's emissions will be more than double that of the biggest emitter, the United States."

Looking again at Jet, he stated in no uncertain tone, "I don't give a damn what our standings are or how much we pollute but I am beginning to think our people do and we need to keep our eye on that aspect." Skipping down the report he added, just listen to this," An overriding priority of all levels of Chinese government is economic growth.

Economic growth underlies poverty alleviation, social stability and ultimately, government legitimacy. The problem is more acute as the country continues trying to improve the livelihood of some 157 million, of its citizens, that still live on less than two dollars per day." Pausing and looking at his companion President Hu continued, "And now to the best part", reading again he continued, "It is hardly surprising, therefore, that the Chinese Government rejects the idea that it should act on climate change out of any kind of moral obligation to other countries, especially since developed countries' historical emissions are larger than China's"

Jet gave his leader a cocked head, twisted mouth look and the President jumped in, "Don't you see we don't have to do anything but parrot their climate control platitudes because 157 million of our people live on what the average American spends on one cup of coffee per day. The west and their decadent, imperialistic systems have caused the problem, whereas our peoples use of the planets energy, on a per capita basis, is not even on the radar scope. Understand?"

Nodding that he followed the President's thought line and continuing to looked concerned he waited and then the President continued, "We will just smile, support all the initiatives put forth, make flattering and supportive speeches and go about our business as usual, when we return home. By the way are you planning to go to Paris with our delegation?"

"No, Yanlin I will use the time to see how young Lin Lee is doing with our Tiger program in America. Think I might like to go visit with our student-agents and see how the plans are going on infiltrating the American protest groups. I am thinking that if Trump should happen to pull it off we could use these groups as a base to throw real anarchy in his path, thereby making his four years so difficult he might have second thoughts about a second term. If we can fill his days with protest, impeachment and chaos he will have less time to be concerned about our market share, the trade deficit or even our fat little friend in Pyongyang."

The President smiled at his old and dear friend and asked, "Ready for lunch in the courtyard?"

"Of course my supreme leader," he said with a mocking smile.

The President just shook his head and looking at the sky asking no one in particular, "Why do I subject myself to you and your humor?"

The two comrades walked out arm-in-arm, glowing with memories and enjoying their special friendship to the max.

CHAPTER
16

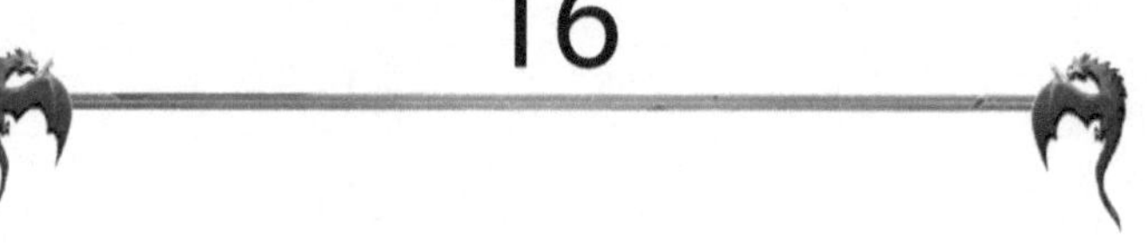

The Chinese ambassador in London notified Jet How's office that a courier had dropped off a report from Christopher Sterling and that the sealed document would be in the embassy secure mail packet that should arrive at Jet's Beijing office by Thursday, December 24, 2015.

Jet read the note that was on top of his stack, when he arrived at his office on Tuesday morning, and ask himself out loud, "Wonder if the smoking gun will hurt, maim or kill?"

Thursday could not come quick enough and looking at his schedule he was pleased to note that the day was free except for a lunch appointment with the Minister of Finance. Thinking about the report he thought, 'Good, that will give me a chance to eat it all in one setting, and I hope there is some real meat and not just noodles.'

Jet was at his office an hour early on Thursday, the day before Christmas and smiled to himself when he thought, 'My world works and the west has been on holiday all week and next week as well. Burying them is a sure thing.'

The packet from Christopher Sterling was a good eight millimeters thick and was encased in a leather-like pouch that was sealed with wax. Jet carefully opened the package and attached to the outside report cover was a invoice and a short letter from the author which was brief and to the point.

"To: Jet How Chung

From: C.S.

Dear Sir,

Here is the report you requested along with my invoice for the balance due as well as detail on the necessary extra expenses which amounted to less than 100K U.S. Dollars. If you have questions my private e-mail address is written on the back of my attached business card. Thank you again for this opportunity to be of service.

C.S."

Jet picked up the report, leafed through the pages, sat it down on the corner of his desk after removing the invoice and pushed the intercom button. "May Ling please come in."

The door opened almost immediately and Jet's long time aide and secretary entered the room and crossed over to her bosses desk. Jet looked up, handed her the invoice and ask, "Remember the 5 million dollar check I took to London with me?"

"Yes, Comrade."

"Well have another identical check, same maker etc., prepared for 5.1 million and send it by courier to the Ambassador in London, in a sealed format and ask him to deliver it to Mr. Sterling. Thank you and no interruptions until my noon appointment."

"Of course Comrade, as you wish."

Jet picked up the report and made his way to the couch in front of the fireplace, sat down and began the long anticipated read. Just over three hours later, an hour before his lunch guest was due, Jet leaned back closed his eyes and tried to make sense of the documents he held in his lap. There certainly wasn't a smoking gun but Jet could plainly see that it would be very difficult for a Presidential candidate to explain away his seedy and unusual behavior. Bells, lights and rockets went off in the Jet How brain; what if, yes, what if the Chinese ambassador in

Washington fed similar data to the Fushion GPS group and the current administration top guns that I had been courting over the last eight years? That would lend support and credibility to the Sterling report and of course no one in that Washington loop would ever know that the Sterling report had been initiated by China. Between the Sterling report and the leaked information from the Chinese embassy it just might be enough to launch covert governmental actions against the Trump campaign. After mulling it over and over, Jet concluded that there was no flaw in his thought-process. "Go over it one more time," he said out loud and his mind raced the course once again. First, leak data, to the Washington establishment based on the Sterling report. Second, push Sterling to get his report published by some news agency in America. Third, set back and watch the Trump campaign try to deal with similar leaks from dissimilar sources. Fourth, fan the flames by encouraging the Washington elite, that Jet had been courting and funding for the eight Obama years, to investigate the Trump campaign for possible ties to Russia and/or collusion with Russia to rig the election.

The circle was complete. The plan was full proof and if by miracles of miracles Trump happened to win the election all of the above would be used against him, over and over again which would amount to Trump being on defense for his full four years. Jet pondered and thought, 'If everyday you are fighting the wolves, nipping at your heels, you certainly won't have much time to worry about China.'

An evil smile came over Jet's face and he pronounced out loud, "There is a smoking gun Mr. Trump; bullet one is on the way and the balance will arrive shortly. Bang, Bang you're dead!"

CHAPTER
17

t was a few minutes before midnight in London when Christopher Sterlings ipad announced that he had an incoming e-mail on his private secure line.

The young lady of the evening had just departed the agent's town house, in an upscale London neighborhood, and Christopher was enjoying the fire and the afterglow of an evening of fine wine, fine food and fine company.

The message was from Jet How read:

'Data received. Balance due can be picked up at recent meeting place. You will be contacted shortly. Suggest you use non public entrance. Code words to older male employee are, do you have any maps of the silk road trade routes?' You may sell data to GPS or any other USA buyer and suggest you try to get copies into the hands of the Directors or their assistants of FBI, CIA, DIA, NSA, NRO, MA, ONSI, INR & TFI. Also request you get some news outlet to publish data. Finally: Mr. Sterling, we have never met.'

A cold chill went up the ex-British agent's back as the last sentence sunk in and visions of Chinese assassin squads danced in his head.

He quickly shrugged it off, realizing that the ten million might just be the tip of the iceberg. He had captured the golden goose and he could sell the eggs as many times as possible. What a turn of events.

He quickly poured himself another scotch and looking into the fire announced out loud, "Here's to Jet How and the golden goose."

Smiling to himself the retired agent thought, 'Let's see you foot dance your way out of this, Mr. Trump.'

CHAPTER
18

The private jet completed the flight from Hawaii in record time as the winds across the Pacific pushed it well beyond its Mach .085 rating of 904 kilometers per hour and the touch down at McCarran Field, almost in downtown Las Vegas, was smooth as silk.

Jet loved coming to Las Vegas and he always marveled at the city of lights setting in the middle of what looked like an endless desert, spotted here and there with bare rock mountains of every size, shape and color.

January in the desert was a beautiful time with clear skies, tempered sun and hundreds of heavenly bodies of every size shape and hue to help pass the time. The number one Bellagio limousine pulled up and parked at the bottom of the plane's stairs as Jet and his staff deplaned into the warm desert breeze.

The ride to the hotel was less than fifteen minutes and a side entrance check-in meant the visiting dignitary did not have to rub elbows with the common folk, but was whisked away to the Presidential Suite by a staff that knew every trick to make their charges feel welcomed and comfortable. Chilled champagne in the private elevator served by a oriental hostess that could knock your socks off from across the room, was just the start. Jet was duly impressed and the hundred dollar bills, he handed out as tips, were gratefully received by the swarming staff.

The suite tour by the head concierge had just completed when Jet's cell phone vibrated and Jet saw that Lin Lee was on the line. "Lin, I just arrived. Are you nearby?"

"Yes, Sir, just down a floor."

"Give me an hour to unpack and freshen up and then meet me at the Lago Restaurant, say about six."

"Yes, Comrade I will be there."

Jet's, personal valet was already laying out a change of fresh clothing as Jet stripped down and headed for the shower as the plumeria leis that the Honolulu embassy people had heaped on him had left him feeling sticky all the way across the Pacific.

The Bellagio's Logo restaurant, run by Executive Chef Julian Serrano was one of Jet's favorite venues. In a private dining room looking out on the always active Bellagio fountains, Jet and Lin Lee were treated to an unbelievable feast of Italian fare. No place in Venice or Porto Fina or for that matter, in all of Italy, could compare with the culinary experience that was available under Chef Serrano's supervision.

With dessert gone and a half empty bottle of Churchill's Tawny Port still waiting to be consumed, Jet finally asked his young associate, "So Lin, how goes the war?"

Taken back by the out of the blue question, Lin stammered and then catching his breath smiled at his mentor and replied, "The outcome is yet to be decided, but the early battles and skirmishes are going well. I have made contact with the top five on your list and have been able to meet with each group's national leadership and in all cases they have been excited about our offer of help and financing. Think the financing, in all cases, was the tipping point."

Jet smiled and replied, "Yes, they all seem to like green dollars and I have always found that the dollars come first and their ideologies come second, although they would have you believe it is just the opposite. Are you familiar with the English word, idiosyncrasy?"

"No, I am not."

"Well it applies to most of the people you will encounter in the academic world, those who believe that their way of thinking and their thought processes are unlike any other and therefore their thinking is unique and far superior to that of their peers. Understand?"

"Yes, yes of course. Everyone of the leaders I have spoken with think that their view of the world is the only true and valid one and that everyone, outside their circle or sphere of influence, is out of step."

With a stern eye piercing look that demanded Lin's complete attention, Jet leaned across the table and said softly, "Lin, tread lightly as you have just described the government you serve."

Jet leaned back in his chair, took a sip of the magnificent thirty-year-old port and waited for his charge to finish digesting the pearl of wisdom he had just imparted.

Lin was truly perplexed. What was Jet trying to tell him? Had he overstepped, was he in a compromising position, would his powers be stripped away and he would ride a desk in some dusty, dirty outback venue where his rotting was not even noticed or would he and all his blood be wiped off the planet? Ancestors help me, what do I do? Beads of perspiration dotted the young man's forehead and Jet smiled, knowing that once again he had total control over every aspect of the life form that sat in front of him. The raw power was his source of energy and without explanation or apology he stood up and asked, "Want to watch me win some big money?"

Lin came back from his side trip to hell, dabbed his forehead with the fine linen napkin and forcing a smile replied, "Of course Comrade."

As the two men departed Lago's and headed for the gaming area Jet said, "How about breakfast in my room tomorrow morning about eight. That way we can discuss details without any interruptions."

"Sounds good, I will be there at eight with all my files."

"I am partial to roulette: have a little system that seems to work for me. I have convinced myself that if I divide the wheel into fourths then my odds are one in four rather than one in thirty-five. So starting at double zero, I go nine numbers to the left which on most wheels means I am covering 1, 36, 3, 34 and 5 red and 13, 24, 15 and 22 black plus double zero. Each turn of the wheel I cover each of the above numbers and I like to play the black chips so my outlay on each trip of the ball is one thousand dollars. If any of the numbers hit my payout is three thousand five hundred dollars. It can get interesting and I like the relative slow pace of the game. The other table games like craps and blackjack just move too fast for me."

Lin watched Jet for an hour or so as the system seemed to be working in that Jet had traded over half his hundred dollar black chips for 500 dollar chips and the pit boss was hovering in the area. Jet removed ten of the 500 chips and handed them to Lin and said, "Go play awhile. I'll see you in the morning."

Lin, big eyed, started to refuse the offer, but the smile behind the extended hand said, "Do as you are told!", and Lin took the chips and made a hasty retreat. As he walked away fingering the five thousand dollars, he ask himself if he should put it away for a rainy day or blow it. Rainy day won as he found the cashier cage and converted the chips to a stack of hundred dollar bills which was too big for his wallet and had to be folded and stuffed in his coat pocket. He felt like every criminal in the world was watching him as he made his way to safety of his room.

As advertised, Jet was seated at a large antique table next to a picture window, drinking hot tea when Lin arrived a few minutes before eight. Jet waved him to a seat and said to the butler, please bring him whatever he wants and then we would like you and your staff to leave." The seasoned employee nodded his understanding and ask, "What can I bring you sir?"

"Just coffee for now. I ate earlier. Thank you."

Coffee appeared and the staff departed quickly.

Jet smiled at his guest and ask, "Are you ready to share your secrets with me comrade?"

"Of course," Lin said as he paused to sip his coffee. "I assumed your list was built in order of importance so I will start with Occupy Wallstreet. The original protest was called for by Kalle Lasn and others of Adbusters, a Canadian anti-consumerist publication, who conceived of a September 17 occupation in lower Manhattan. The first such proposal appeared on the Adbusters web site on February 2, 2011. Various other groups picked up the idea and because Zuccotti Park was not city property it was chosen as the site. Mayor Bloomberg had said, early on, that people have the right to protest and that set the tone for the occupation by the 99% as they called themselves. The one percent was of course the Wall Street businesses that OWS demanded share their wealth, get out of politics, submit to bank reform, forgiveness of student loans and a whole litany of other monetary demands. I have meet with Lasn, and several others and right now I don't have a firm grasp of what they have planned for the future, but I can tell you that they are all anti-Trump to the core and none of them felt that he would be the Republican candidate and if he was that Hillary would beat him in a landslide. My assessment is that they are a group of out-of-touch academia's that really don't have a plan, but I think if Trump was the nominee you will see them regenerate. I plan to follow their activities and have our cells at Columbia University, New York University and Barnard College actively working with OWS and their leadership so I am certain that we will be able to influence their future actions."

Jet nodded understanding as he finished a waffle with strawberry topping and piles of whipped cream that had been getting cold.

Lin continued, "The second group, Black Lives Matter will be the most important group, at least that is my current opinion. They have the media in the palm of their hand and all the guilt-ridden white people will rally to their causes, especially those that think of themselves as 'white privileged', and that would be most of the student population on most of the colleges and universities in the nation. They have been made to feel guilty by the educational process and by quotas which give black students preference over white students, solely on the basis of race. Most of the white students come from middle-class American homes where hard working parents only want the best for their darling children. They mortgage the farm to send the kiddies off to prestigious colleges and universities so that the degree they come home with will open job opportunity doors and they will be more successful than their parents and of course success is measured by income. The parents want their kids to be successful, rich and socially prominent in the upscale white communities where they live. Black Lives has made this dream seem evil because it is in such sharp contrast to the black family where each child in a family unit may have a different father and where poverty and racial injustice is shoved in their face on a daily basis."

Lin paused to finish his coffee and then continued, "The founders were Patrisse Cullors, Alicia Garza and Opal Tometi and I have met with all three and they are thrilled to have our support. They have thirty chapters around the country and I am in the process of matching up each chapter with a one of our local college cells and I would say that within three to four months our agents will have infiltrated their organization. I have promised each chapter financial aid and special aid to the founders. It is possible that I will spend at least a quarter of my budget within the Black Lives Matter movement, provided you agree."

"Well, Lin it seems like you have given this a great deal of thought and while it is not prudent to put all your eggs in one basket, I have to say that your argument seems sound. This white guilt thing is something that I would not have expected but I can see that to the do gooders of the world it would be an important step on the way to racial equality, which of course will never happen, but which we shall support with our time and money. Yes, go ahead with your plans and give Black Lives Matter your full support and bring it to the top of the list. Understand?"

"Yes, I will Comrade and in that regard we are starting on a campaign to paint Donald Trump as a sexist racists which will almost guarantee that the black population will give him very little support and that the female population will reject him as well; after all women make up 55% of the electorate. If he should happen to be the Republican candidate he will not beat a woman whose husband once said he was America's first black President. It all adds up to odds that can't be beat, don't you agree?"

"I do, and I am also tired. I played late last night and I have been invited out tonight by the hotel management so I am going to be ready for a rest between now and then. I don't think you need to go into any further detail. I will tell the President how well we chose and that you are carrying out your assignment at the highest levels of proficiency. Have a good trip home and the President and I thank you for your hard work and dedication."

Lin Lee bowed to his senior and quickly exited the plush surroundings, went down to his room, removed the five thousand dollars from the wall safe and prepared to "go crazy" for just once in his life. After all he was part of the Presidents' inner circle and the toughest man in China had just paid him a supreme complement and would not, he was sure, begrudge him a good time in the sin capital of the world.

CHAPTER
19

A week later, Jet was all smiles as he changed out of his work clothes into silk lounging pajamas and looked forward to a relaxing evening at home. Just a few days ago a Washington cable news outlet, Buzzfeed, had published the Sterling report and it was the talk of the world. The subject of the report seemed unruffled by all the attention and had, thus far, been able to sidestep most of the damming data by declaring it fake news. Jet was sure that over the long term it would turn out to be his Achilles heel, especially if he could get some of the Americans intelligence agencies to launch investigations of the candidate and his staff based on the report and on the data the Embassy staff was leaking to every one of their American agency contacts. The Chinese government had, during the Obama years, spent millions to wine and dine the American agencies heads and their assistants, to say nothing of the sweetheart deals that Jet had worked out with the vice-president's son and extended family members. Jet anticipated that the money spent would now reap rewards as the government officials, that he and the ambassador frequently contacted, seemed to be, largely Trump haters, of the first magnitude.

A light dinner of pork based pot stickers and his favorite fried rice had been followed by the world's best sake which Jet bought by the case at 216,000 yen (US$2800) per bottle. It was Hokusetsu Daiginjo UYK35 Shizkuzake titanium gold that came in a tear drop shaped bottle and it just happened to be the President's favorite drink, as well.

Jet's household staff had been in high gear for days as the President was having dinner with Jet, in his home, tomorrow night and everything would be perfect. The President loved getting away from his staff and family to share quality time with his favorite elder, friend and confidante. It was the one place in the world where he could let his hair down and be totally himself without worrying about the duties and the responsibilities of his job. If he wanted to drink too much and shout from the rooftops, he could do it with impunity within Jet's palatial compound where the servants knew that to breathe a word could mean disappearance from the known world. It had happened once, and the punishment was swift and with malice aforethought. A violated trust meant the perpetrator and his extended family would disappear from the planet as Jet's special forces security guards were not held accountable for any action, they deemed necessary to safeguard their employer.

With another decanter of the warm white lighting under his belt Jet reviewed his new proposal, for the umpteenth time, to make sure that when presented, the President could not ask any question that Jet could not answer. The anticipation was almost more than he could bear but he knew that he must be calm and present his plan in the simplest form possible.

Thinking out loud Jet rehearsed his presentation for what he hoped was the last time. "Comrade President did you know that we currently manufacture about eighty-two percent of all the shipping containers used in the world and that Chinese cargo handlers move over 715,000 containers per day or about thirty percent of the global traffic?" The President will smile at me and ask, "Where is this going Jet and why do I need to know these boring statistics?"

I will continue by saying, Comrade our containers are in every country of the world. They are at loading docks, in warehouses, on mile-long trains crisscrossing almost every corner of every country and they are on thousands of ships plying the oceans blue or tied to docks in almost every world port. He will give me that look and ask again, "Why do I need to know the obvious. I travel, I see; what's the point old friend?"

'I will continue by saying, Comrade President, if we start now, we can have over thirty million containers scattered around the world by mid 2020, each with four liters of dragon, excuse me, I mean tiger gas hidden in each container's four support columns. The hollow steel columns can contain a compressed gas cylinder, with a release mechanism that can be triggered from satellites and that way we can release our tiger on a country by country basis; whenever we see fit.'

'He may ask, what happens if a container is lost at sea or damaged in an accident and the cylinders are discovered? The cylinder is made from oriented polypropylene which is a very tough plastic membrane which will rupture at any depth over twenty fantoms. If the container is in an accident and ripped open the four heavy gauge steel corner posts could be bent or mangled but they would never break open to reveal the thin plastic liner on the inside. The receiving-tracking chip is no bigger than a large button and is bonded to the inside of the top corner brackets which are pieces of cast steel which could also never break open. They might bend or be smashed but would never break open to reveal the chip.'

'He will, of course, give me a incredulous look, shake his head and ask, "How do you come up with this stuff Jet?"

'I will just smile and offer him more sake.' The next day's dinner was a roaring success in that the President allowed himself the luxury of letting go, enjoying the comradeship and of course being amazed at the never ending stream of diabolical schemes that exited Jet's head. The details of this most recent plan were explained, expanded, refined and implemented over the next months and by year end every finished container, with a Made in China label, contained four pressurized cylinders, hidden within the structural steel corner support posts along with a small activating transmitter. A special secret agency, that reported only to Jet, and was housed next to his Beijing office, was formed that did nothing but track these new containers. A special global tracking satellite was launched that would not only facilitate the tracking but could also trigger release of the dragon breath gases from each individual container.

CHAPTER
20

President Hu and Jet How Chung had just finished an early breakfast and were now seated in the communications center near the President's office, watching the lead into the national debate between Hillary Clinton, Bernie Sanders and Martin O'Malley. It was 8 p.m. in Charleston and 8 a.m. the next day in Beijing and the big show was almost ready to begin.

The anchor was busy puffing himself up so he would not miss his fifteen minutes of fame. Clinton was in her usual big-hip pants suit, Bernie looked his disheveled best, and Martin O'Malley just as well not been on the stage as it was clear his candidacy was on the edge of a cliff with nowhere to go but down.

The three candidates all played the race card invoking the memories of Dr. King and before they finished their embellishments you would have thought the good doctor did indeed walk on water.

Jet and President Hu snickered out loud when Clinton was asked what she would do in her first hundred days. Her predictable fluff-fluff answer was, "I would work quickly to present to the Congress my plans for creating more good jobs in the manufacturing, infrastructure, clean and renewable energy, and raising the minimum wage and finally guaranteeing equal pay for women's work."

Jet How whispered to his comrade in arms, "Yes, and by the way I will transfer more American jobs to China as they are a poor nation that needs our help." President Hu doubled over and had to retrieve his white handkerchief to wipe away the tears of laughter.

"You are too much old friend, don't know if I can stand any more of your critiques and I don't know about you but I can't take anymore of this dribble. Are you going to watch the whole thing?"

"I'll put in a few more minutes and if there is any exciting news I will be sure you are the first to hear."

President Hu left the booth and headed back to his office as Jet settled in for a boring morning.

Clinton and Sanders traded barbs over the gun issue and Jet was amused that they were both really on the same page; i.e. repeal the second amendment. Jet smiled to himself as he remembered that he had worked hard to get guns out of the hands of the Chinese masses and he was certain that had that not been done, China would have spent the last forty years in a state of constant turmoil. Remembering back to the recent events at Wuhan he thought, 'If those people had guns there would most likely have been a different outcome.'

The remainder of the show covered crime, policing, and the Affordable Care Act and neither Jet, nor the American public, learned anything new.

As Jet made his way back to his office, he compared what he had just watched with the last Republican debate and thought, 'I still think Trump will be the Republican candidate and I would bet my last yuan that he will beat either one of those socialist fools. We can spend billions to fight him but in the final analysis the American people, outside Washington and the liberal population centers, will have the last word and we need to plan for that eventuality.'

In an e-mail to President Hu, reporting on various projects, including the highly secret tiger-container project Jet pontificated to his leader, You didn't miss anything. Just posturing fools displaying their utter contempt for the deplorable masses while the elephant in the room, ie. Donald Trump, seems to be marching to the tune that the American people are singing. It is going to be interesting and I am more than ever convinced that Trump will be the next President regardless of how much money we allocate to defeat him. By the way, the polls, right up to election eve will show Hillary winning but don't be taken in as a Clinton, that we can manipulate, will not be the next American President."

During the run-up to the Democratic convention Jet and President Hu spent time together watching the show and every day Jet became more and more convinced that their worst fear was about to be realized, as he had been predicting since the get-go.

In early July it was official. Hillary beat out Bernie and the Bernieites yelled foul but Hillary just smiled and prepared to become the 45th President of the United States, following in her husband's footsteps.

Meanwhile the Republican convention, near the end of July, had its share of drama in that many major republicans announced far and wide that they would not attend. Both Bush Presidents declined, as did John McCain and Bob Dole along with a host of republican senators such as Rob Portman of Ohio, Ben Sasse of Nebraska, Jeff Flake of Arizona and the list continued.

As Jet predicted it was a Trump landslide and the commentators like Howard Kirk and many others had to eat their words. Trump was the candidate and his race against the coronation of queen Hillary would be of epic proportions.

Jet noted that companies like Wells Fargo, UPS, Motorola, JP Morgan Chase, Ford all announced they would not fund or sponsor the Republican convention and when Apple jumped on the bandwagon many of the pundits doubled down on their predictions that Trump could never win. Jet concluded that the more they rode Trump into the ground the more the American people would rally around him. In America the underdog always had the common man's support and Trump was the underdog of underdogs.

Friday, August fifth found Jet and President Hu at the bunker compound where they were taking lunch in the courtyard, just prior to their group of five meeting that would commence the next day.

The conversation had briefly covered the tiger-container project but was now focused on the events in America and what it meant to China's long range plans.

"Are you still convinced that Trump will win?" the President asked, as he looked up from his lunch and gave Jet a cool calculating stare.

"If I was a betting man, I would bet you my entire stock, eight cases, of Hokusetsu sake. How's that for being sure Comrade President," Jet replied with a twinkle in his eye.

"Really, you are that sure?"

"Yes, and there is just one reason."

"And what might that be Comrade?"

"Simple; he is not a politician. He is a business man and he says it like it is and that my leader is what the American public wants to hear. All the mumble jumble from Hillary is just fluff and the people know it and they will reward Mr. Trump. You can take it to the bank."

Jet refolded his linen napkin, placed it carefully by his empty soup bowl, pushed his chair back from the table and announced, "And now my President with your approval I shall go take my nap so I will be bright eyed for tomorrow's important meeting."

"Permission granted as I understand that older people must get their rest."

Jet unseated himself, walked around the table and placing his hand on the Presidents shoulder said, "You truly are a magnanimous leader."

CHAPTER 21

The unusual Saturday meeting started promptly at eight a.m. with all in attendance except General Zhao Keshi who had recently been diagnosed with lung cancer and was not up to the trip from his home in Beijing. President Hu explained the situation to the members and stated, "We will need to find a replacement for the General. I have some ideas as I have had several interviews with the General's aide, a Vice General named Fan Chang Long. The Vice General was delegated the Tiger project by General Keshi when he first found out he was terminal, with my approval. If there is no objection I shall include the Vice General Long in our next meeting. If any of you have first-hand knowledge I would appreciate your comments, otherwise the selection will be affirmed."

Jet asked, "Comrade, I know Vice General Long and I am certain that he could fit into our group and be a valuable asset. I think he went to college in America and he may bring us a unique prospective."

"Yes Jet, you are correct. If there are no other comments, I will ask the Vice General, who will shortly be a full General, to join us at our next meeting which shall be in late October. The exact date will be announced. Jet would you like to tell the group what you have been up to?"

"Of course Comrade President." Looking around the table, Jet made eye contact with each person and then said, "I have come to the realization that America will shortly be a full blown antagonist under their new leadership. We are mounting an incredible campaign and Lin Lee is doing a fantastic job infiltrating the protest organizations in America but I am afraid it will fall short. Yes, I am predicting that Donald Trump will be the next President and I wish it were not true but this is my head speaking not my heart. Comrades, America under a Trump administration will be a great deal different than the last 24 years under Clinton, Bush and Obama where our expansion met little if any resistance. We took over the Panama Canal, we have become the second largest economy in the world, we have kept America in its place by threating to unleash the little munch-kin in Pyongyang and his nuclear arsenal. We have built our off-shore defense islands and we have captured the world's economy on the backs of our workers. This did not happen by chance. It happened because we made a plan and then worked the plan and worked it to perfection. The Rainbow Zhanlue was important, it got us where we are, but the Tiger Zhanlue will bring it all to a new level and it makes little difference how hard America and Trump push back. We will win this battle and the resulting war and you comrades have front row seats, so sit back and enjoy the performance. I wish I could share a new secret project that has recently been implemented but suffice to say, you will see America and the world on their knees and Comrades we owe it all to the foresight and clear thinking that President Hu has brought to our time and our country."

The members, caught up in Jet's narrative, jumped to their feet and clapped and clapped and clapped. President Hu finally stood, acknowledged their standing ovation and moved around the table shaking each man's hand and thanking him for his work and dedication. Last was Jet and the President said so all could hear. "We would not be in this position if it was not for this diabolical rascal." Clapping broke out again as the two men embraced and then returned to their seats.

"Comrades, thank you. Lin do you have a report on the medical supply issues?"

"Thank you Comrade President," Lin said as he stood to address the group. "My previous report told you we had hundreds of Chinese companies scouring the world for health-related companies to buy, merge or offer sweetheart deals if they would move their manufacturing facilities to China. That number has now gone to over fifteen hundred and the support staff of 4,000 has been almost doubled. There is not a segment of the health industry that we are not chasing, from bandaids to full-body scanning machines. It's remarkable what we are finding and as promised I have a report for each of you that shows our percentage of market share of each major and minor sub-grouping. For instance right now we have about 28 percent of the world's antibiotic manufacturing capability, but with the new acquisitions planned that number will by year end be close to 40 percent and by 2019 it will be in the 85 to 90 percent bracket. You will note in the report that for each sub-group you are given an estimated percentage in black numbers followed by a red number. The red number is our projection for the end of 2019. Budget wise we are beginning to approach our limit but we anticipate that the increased sales volume will bring in offsetting revenue. Questions?"

"Thank you Comrade, keep up the good work. Since we don't have a report from General Keshi, I guess you are last on the list Admiral Wanguan."

"Thank you Comrade President. I certainly don't have dramatic results to point to, like Comrade Lin, but we are making progress. We are cataloging all marginal lands, lands that today produce nothing because of their location or because of the lack of water, inadequate soil types, etc. We are coming up with maps that will show where we can expand food production provided the technologies can be worked out and put into practice. Our scientists are brilliant and they are finding new ways to approach almost every problem that the agriculture industry faces. Just one example that may interest you involves the Yellow River which is 5464 km. long and which has been called the cradle of Chinese civilization. The river carries the highest level of sediment concentration on earth, and we are looking at ways to pump some of it's flow into remote valleys, let the sediments settle out, thereby creating land areas that can grow crops. It is a long-term solution but this and many other amazing technology advancements are being made daily and it will all work to help us solve the overall puzzle. Questions?"

Jet asked, "Comrade, over the centuries has the river's high sediment content always been such?"

"I am not sure Comrade but if I had to guess I would say yes, why do you ask?"

"As I recall the river flows into the Bohai Sea and Bohai bay which is almost circular and if I am not mistaken at least a dozen other rivers also flow into the bay. Would that be correct?"

"Yes, Comrade I am sure you are right."

A pause followed while Jet's mind raced ahead and he finally said, "Since our early history these rivers have been depositing sediment in the bay. Fine soil that I am sure would make any farmer smile. If we dredged the bottom of the bay and build peninsulas extending out from the perimeter of the bay, like spokes of a wheel, we could create thousands of hectares of new premium farm land. We must have the technology as the military islands we are building in the South China Sea are a combination of dredging and fill."

The Admiral looked at his President and asked, "Do you have him registered as a national treasure?", nodding towards Jet.

The room erupted in laughter and President Hu replied, "Yes, and his brain will be housed in a special section of the National Museum."

Laughter again filled the room and before it subsided the President stood up and said, "Thank you Comrades for your input. Our next meeting will be just before the American elections and I look forward to seeing you at that time. Meeting adjourned."

"Jet, may I see you in my office?"

Jet did not reply but followed his leader out of the conference room and into the sun-filled office. The glass patio doors were open and the waterfall put out a soothing noise that filled the room.

"Jet, will you be traveling between now and our next meeting?"

"I don't have any pressing matters, why do you ask?"

"I want you to spend some time with our new General. Look into his background in detail and make sure he does not have any skeletons in his closet. Understand?"

"Yes, Comrade President, I understand your concerns and the sensitive nature of the Zhanlue and I will make certain that the General brings no surprises."

"Thank you. Are you heading home today?"

"Yes, my wife is ill and I think that the end is near, so yes I am on my way home, but reluctantly, if you know what I mean."

"I am sorry old friend. I know you will miss her. Keep me in the loop."

"Thank you Yanlin and if there is nothing else, I shall take your leave."

"Of course and may our ancestors watch over you."

Jet exited the office through the conference room, gave crisp instructions to his aide, who was waiting near the door, and the two men headed toward the elevators and their waiting plane.

CHAPTER
22

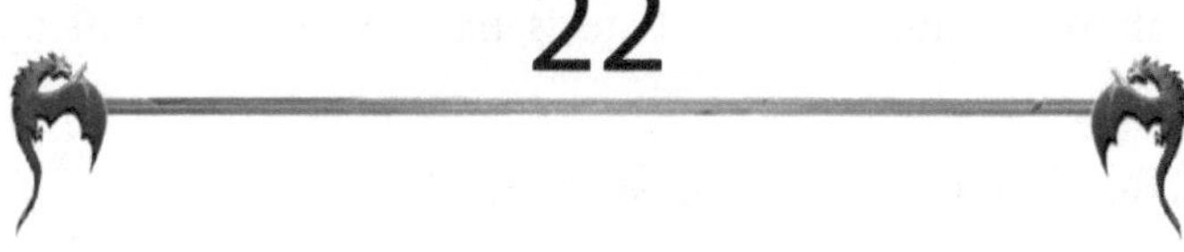

The Chinese Ambassador in Washington was one of the most sought after guests in the D.C. social arena. Senator, Cabinet member or Agency head all felt like they had just hit a world series home run if Xu Qiliang and his wife were on their guest list.

The ambassador was a large man for a Chinese, standing over six foot four inches tall and his rugged Mongolian features and year around tan complexion put most of the ladies in a twitter. He had held the ambassadorship position since 2006 and was now pushing sixty but his hard athletic body and his fame on the tennis court made him appear much younger.

His wife, Maling was a stunning oriental beauty and it was rumored that she had a spare bedroom at the Embassy filled with rack after rack of the finest oriental silk dresses. She was as classy as beautiful and her list of admirers included almost every major American politician and even some past presidents, one of which who actually suggested, in her delicate ear, that she might enjoy an evening with him.

The couple churned the D.C. social circuit during President Hu's Rainbow Zhanlue/Obama ramp-up and were instrumental in making the Zhanlue such a success. Treasury secretaries, FBI directors and all the lesser players, in between, were frequent guests at the Chinese Embassy and to be included was considered a major social coup.

During the Obama years when Jet How's friend General Liu had been buying up almost 1.1 trillion in U.S. Treasury bonds the Ambassador had been his closest confidant and the General made sure that the Ambassador's Swiss bank account received periodic deposits that the people in the Peoples Republic would never see. Retirement on the French Riviera or Bora Bora or wherever the Ambassador's fancy might lead him was assured.

Early July in D.C. was hot and humid and Jet hated being a slave to air conditioning but it was important to give the Ambassador just a taste of the new Zhanlue so that he would understand the importance of the Sterling report.

The Ambassador had set aside the whole day for the President's hatchet-man and while he enjoyed Jet's company he was always on guard because Jet's reputation proceeded him wherever he went. The latest rumors about some sort of massacre in Wuhan was currently circling the government institutions and it had everyone in the power grid on the edge of their seats. Jet had of course planted the rumors so that the Chinese officials around the world would know what a long arm he had. He always felt more secure when the underlings were fearful, it was just what he did.

Jet came down from his fourth story apartment, in the embassy complex, accompanied by the Ambassador's private secretary who led him to the sanctuary and security of his private office.

Jet was greeted with, "Comrade Chung, so good to see you again. I hope your flight went well and that the accommodations are to your liking."

"Yes, Xu, everything is fine, just fine and I bring you direct greetings from your President."

"Thank you and my regards when you next see his excellency."

"So old friend, are you here for the social aspects of Washington or do we have more serious matters to discuss?"

"The latter and I would ask that if your jamming technology is not up and running, that you turn it on as what I have to say is rated a top state secret."

"We are fully covered in this room so say what you like, please."

"Xu, over the past year a new top secret Zhanlue has been initiated by the President and a small group of his closest advisers. You will remember the Rainbow Zhanlue which was child's play when compared to the current Zhanlue. I cannot even give you a name but I can tell you that if you wish to discuss any aspect of what goes on here today you can use the code word 'tiger' when communicating with either the President or myself. We will immediately know the subject and will address your comments or questions. Understood?"

"Yes, Comrade, understood."

"Good, Here is a report from a British agent about Mr. Trump. I want you to read it carefully and digest all the data given. I then want you to develop a series of similar stories, with similar timeframes that could have been generated by our world-wide spy network." Jet stopped as he noticed a frown of non-understanding on the Ambassador's face and started again, "Xu, our goal is to do everything within our power to deny Donald Trump the presidency of the United States. No more, no less. So, this report is one source and the intelligence community in America will judge it knowing it is just one source. We want to help them with their judgment by giving them additional data from completely unrelated sources. Now they will have two sources and it will elevate the report and give it more credence. Do you understand that?"

"Yes, I can see that if you have a report and then it is verified by a second, completely independent report, that it makes the first report more believable. Is that the essence of what you are saying?"

"Exactly. Yes, and as you are reporting the details of our networks independent investigations you will be passing on other data as well such as, number one - we understand that there may be a communication line open between Trump and Putin, two - we think it is possible that Russia and Trump are trying to tamper with the US elections, three – we have heard that Trump may be in collusion with Russia to help steal the election from Hillary, four- it is possible that General Flynn, Paul Manafort, Roger Stone and Carter Page are in on the collusion and last, there may be some kind of dirty tricks going on in Ukraine that they should be investigated as well." Pausing Jet looked at his subordinate and asked, "Are you following me Ambassador?"

"Yes, Comrade I understand, but this does not seem to rise anywhere near the level of activity that the Rainbow Zhanlue created. I don't understand why this is so top secret but then maybe I don't need to understand."

"Look Xu what I have given you is just the tip of the iceberg. Let me give you a little of the overall picture. It shall be sketchy, with no real details but maybe it will increase your understanding so that you can better carry out your assignment. OK?"

"Yes."

"Let's say that everyone in Washington is wrong and Donald Trump becomes the next President. He will not be a Clinton, a Bush or a Obama. He will make life extremely difficult for our country and our regime; he will be like no other and since he can't be bought he will be a real thorn in our side. I can see him ripping up trade deals, bring back the US military, thwarting us at every turn and being rash enough to take on that troll in Pyongyang. He will be a nightmare, so to help insure he does not win we are initiating this little campaign. We have several more streets we will chase him down and hope they all come together with his defeat on November 8." Pausing, Jet looked deep into the ambassadors eyes and said very quietly, "I, however, think that whatever we do will not be enough. I will bet that he pulls off the upset of upsets and that means we will have to deal with him for the next four years. That's not acceptable so we need to cut his reign short and one way to do that is to hit him big with Russian collusion and election tampering. We will use our money, our classified information and our Democratic friends and Democratic agency heads and anything else to sabotage his presidency. I guarantee you major players will be calling for his impeachment even before he is sworn in and with proper nudging Obama will launch investigations, before he departs, that will haunt Mr. Trump for every day of his first and only term. Now the top secret part."

Jet stood up and paced the room and coming back he stood directly in front of the Ambassador and with his penetrating eyes flashing continued, "If all the above fails, and he survives collusion with Russia and Ukraine, impeachment, scandal and unrelenting attacks on his wife and children, we will, before the 2020 election, ensure he is not reelected. I cannot give you the details but know that a great scourge will grip not only America but the entire planet in early 2020 and this one event will seal the coffin on his reelection."

The Ambassadors eyes were as big as saucers. He was almost out of breath but heard himself saying, "Comrade will this affect my wife and children?"

"Yes, it will affect every human on the planet but I promise you will not be in this assignment one day of 2020. You will have been transferred back home by late 2019, so rest easy and Comrade do not share this with anyone, not your wife, your children, absolutely no one. Understood?"

The 'understood' was delivered with piercing black eyes that one would expect to see coming from the leader of a firing squad and it was not lost on the Ambassador Xu. He 'understood', he would comply or he would die, of that he was certain.

CHAPTER
23

The TV room off President Hu's office had a fifteen-meter diameter and a double seated couch in the center that rotated 360 degrees. The President could watch news shows from around the world. All he had to do was press the remote, built into the arm of the chair, for the country he wanted to watch and if by magic all the previous days news reports from that country, with Chinese interpreters dubbed in over the original audio feed, came into view.

In addition, if any one of his ambassadors, around the world, wanted to leave the President a message they could do so. None of the messages could contain any requests for contact or information, but rather were informative narratives that the ambassadors deem interesting and important information about the country in which they were based. Each ambassador usually left only 60 to 90-second messages, so it was easy for the President to flash through the major countries on the list and come away with a fair understanding of what was going on around the world. Today, however, each TV was tuned into America and every cable and network entity from the land of the free was broadcasting the Republican national convention. The Vice Presidential candidate Mike Pence was speaking and Jet nudged the President at the conclusion of his opening remarks and whispered, "Listen carefully comrade as he is describing their next President."

The two men did listen as Pence opened, "You have nominated a man for President who never quits, who never backs down, a fighter, a winner. Until now he has had to do it all by himself against all odds. But this week, with this united party, he has got back-up." The crowd roared and he continued, "Let's resolve here and now that Hillary Clinton will never become the President of the United States of America," and the crowd roared its wholehearted approval.

President Hu, hit the mute button and looked at Jet and said, "Well so far you are right on target, but do you really believe he can beat the queen?"

"Not many of the soothsayers in America think it is possible and the polls are all stacked in her favor but between now and November 8 you will see dedication that we all can envy. He will out-work her every hour of every day and like the soon to be Vice President said, he will never quit."

"But he can't win without the black vote and the women vote and I understand he is running far behind in both categories. I even saw a clip the other day where Hillary was talking to a black audience and she started impersonating them by using their language and terms. She knows how to work the crowd and Bill will be there rooting her on and we both know he is a master at framing the truth to suit his needs."

"All you say is true but mark my words, if Hillary holds one rally per day, she will think she is overworked, while in the meantime Trump will be doing three per day and flying all night to get to the first rally of the next day."

By the time they finished their review the President was in full stride, accepting the nomination and vowing to beat Hillary.

The two men sat in silence as they watch Mr. Trump outline his vision of America. One segment caught their collective attention when he said, "I am going to bring our jobs back to Ohio and to America, and I am not going to let companies move to other countries, firing their employees along the way, with no consequences. My opponent, on the other hand, has supported virtually every trade agreement that has been destroying our middle class. She supported NAFTA, and she supported China's entrance into the World Trade Organization, another one of her husband's colossal mistakes. She supported the job killing trade deal with South Korea. She has supported the Trans-Pacific Partnership. The TPP will not only destroy our manufacturing, but it will make America subject to the rulings of foreign governments.

I pledge to never sign any trade agreement that hurts workers, or that diminishes our freedom and independence. Instead, I will make individual deals with individual countries. No longer will we enter into these massive deals, with many countries that are thousands of pages long and which no one from our country even reads or understands. We are going to enforce all trade violations, including through the use of taxes and tariffs, against any country that cheats. This includes stopping China's outrageous theft of intellectual property, along with their illegal product dumping, and their devastating currency manipulation. Our horrible trade agreements with China and many others will be totally renegotiated."

The President again hit the mute button and looking at Jet ask, "Is that just political bull?"

"No Comrade, that is Donald Trump and he does not engage in normal political discourse. I expect him to win and I expect him to take every promise he has made seriously and as old sailors say, 'batten down the hatches and prepare for the storm of storms.'"

CHAPTER
24

During September and up through mid-October Hillary Clinton and Donald Trump squared off three times and the debates were covered in mind numbing detail by every news organization in the world.

Jet and President Hu watched each one and listened to the soothsayers mostly shred Mr. Trump as they gushed over Hillary's brilliant and super intelligent answers. You could not watch the sparing matches without realizing that the Washington swamp elite, the democratic establishment, the mainstream media and the American people would soundly reject Donald Trump and his brash hip-shooting rhetoric. At least that was the impression that the media would be shouting from the roof tops until about 8 p.m. on election eve.

President Hu keep chiding Jet and questioning his steadfast proclamations that Hillary would lose, and lose by a big enough margin that Trump's victory might even qualify as a mandate, at least in the eyes of the loyal Trumper's.

The second debate in St. Louis was distasteful and made lots of voters, viewers and supporters angry. The locker room charges and Trump's degrading of women were beat into the ground and most viewers yawned and would have urged the moderator to move on to substance. So sometimes people say crude things, we have all done it, but to harp and harp and not let go made many viewers change channels. It was old news and while Trump handled it as best one could he still lost points and President Hu pointed that out to Jet as they watched the soap opera continue to unfold.

Trump was able to bring Bill into the mix and that somewhat put a damper on the sleaze portion of the show. The substance part was lame on both side, with lots of generalities aimed at shoring up each candidates' base.

The final debate was October 19 at the University of Nevada and Chris Wallace was the narrator. Yes, Chris Wallace the FOX news senior anchor whose questions seem to go on forever. He assumes the audience has little or no historical grasp of anything and thus he feels obligated to explain, in mind-numbing detail, every point that could possibly have a bearing on his sciolism question. People all over America scream at their TV's, "What the hell is the question, Chris?"

In a sample of the coverage of the third and final debate by the main stream press, The Atlantic summed it up like this.

"Trump was irritable, blustery, and spouted dishonest statements. Clinton, meanwhile, was workmanlike and studious and found herself occasionally on the defensive over her e-mail server and hacked messages released by WikiLeaks. In general, she seemed content to play it conservative, holding on to what most polls find as a strong lead, rather than aim for a knockout blow. Trump delivered his most substantive and detailed performance, and landed a few solid blows, but as in previous debates, his erratic behavior overshadowed them."

The Atlantic ended its hatchet job with this paragraph.

"The end of the election is looking equally anticlimactic. With less than three weeks to go, Trump is falling behind in the polls. While debates are seldom good places to change the momentum of the race, it was one last chance for Trump to impress upon a huge national audience his readiness for the presidency; instead, he chose to question the very enterprise he wishes to run. If he loses on November 8, there's no reason to expect a friendlier denouement to the election that there was to Wednesday's debate."

The puppet of Putin lines that Hilary and Donald traded prompted President Hu to nudge Jet and ask, "Are you responsible for getting our friend in Moscow into the mix?"

Jet nodded in the affirmative and concentrated on the ongoing banter that characterized the remainder of the proceedings. When Hillary stated, "We have 17 - 17 intelligence agencies, civilian and military, who have all concluded that these espionage attacks, these cyberattacks, come from the highest levels of the Kremlin and they are designed to influence our election, I find that deeply disturbing."

Jet could not help but smirk as each one of the 17 agencies had been on his contact list and the ambassador and Lin Lee must have had done there jobs well. Smiling to himself Jet thought, 'Isn't it amazing what money and whispers can do?'

The big big news that came out of the third debate was when Chris Wallace ask, "I want to asked you on this stage tonight: Do you make the same commitment that you will absolutely--sir, that you will absolutely accept the result of this election?"

Trump replied, "I will look at it at the time. I'm not looking at anything now. I'll look at it at the time."

For the next few minutes they traded barbs, big barbs and Clinton ended up saying, "That's horrifying. You know every time Donald thinks things are not going in his direction, he claims whatever it is , is rigged against him."

Chris finally managed to change the subject but the damage was done and the story of the third debate was, Trump may question the results of the election if it doesn't go his way.

At the end of the show President Hu ask his companion, "Are you still convinced that Trump will win?" "More than ever my President, more than ever."

CHAPTER
25

Friday, October 28 found the group of five at President Hu's office in Beijing, in the conference room that was between his office and the circular newsroom.

Everyone seemed to be in good spirits despite the fact that General Zhao Keshi had just been admitted to intensive care ward of the Oasis International Hospital which was the most luxurious facility in Beijing. The General's prognoses was not good and his comrades all voiced concern. His replacement General Fan Chang Long, was attending his first meeting and the President arranged to be fifteen minutes late so that the other members could get a chance to visit with the new member.

When the President entered the banter stopped and everyone took their designated seat.

"Good morning comrades. Nice to see you all again and a special welcome to our newest member, General Fan Chang Long, which I am going to shorten to General Long."

The General acknowledged his welcome and said, "I am humbled to be in such sterling company and I shall implore my ancestors to give me the wisdom and understanding so that I might contribute to your body of work."

"I am sure you will fit in just fine General Long and we look forward to your contributions. Speaking of which we just as well put you on the hot seat from the beginning, do you have a report ready?"

"Yes, Comrade President, I do. From the beginning of this project, I was General Keski's principal aide and as such I was in the loop and helped the General with the initial startup planning and organizing. I wrote the General's last report and since his sickness I have been looking into someplace in Tibet that we could use as a training ground for our troops. I understand that this was Jet's idea and I thank you comrade for putting forth such an out-of-the-box suggestion."

Jet nodded acceptance of the General's praise and the General continued. In the southeast part of the area known as Xizang Zizhiou, or Tibet, there is a city named Nyingchi, sometimes called Linzhi, that has a population of just over one-hundred thousand. It is located in an area that has been compared to the Swiss Alps. The tallest mountain in the area is Namche Barwa Peak which towers to over 7000 meters. It is also the home of Yarlung Zangbo Grand Canyon which is the largest canyon in the world. It is isolated and since we control the area, I think it would be an ideal training ground. We could send in troops to take over every aspect of the government, on a temporary basis of course, and the hands on training would go a long way toward preparing us to take over countries that may need our leadership in the future. With your approval, I will start drawing up detailed military style occupation plans that will cover every contingency of governmental operation."

The General seated himself and waited.

President Hu smiled at his colleagues and directing his comments to the General asked, "I assume this will be a spring and summer operation so you don't have to fight the winter weather. Will you be ready to move by April of 2017?"

"Yes, Comrade, that can be done."

"Well then keep me in your loop as I think I might want to visit the area in July or August to see how the program plays out."

"Jet, are you ready to tell us what you have been doing?"

"Of course, Comrade. As I detailed at our last meeting we are infiltrating all of the protest movements in America. Our student agents, all 200 thousand of them, have been mobilized and they are working their way into leadership positions in organizations like Black

Lives Matter." Stopping, Jet smiled at his group and with a sly smile asked, "you do know what the letters BLM stand for?" Finally, the new General could not resist and said, "Black Lives Matter, I assume."

"Well yes, but there is another meaning - Burn, Loot and Murder." The conference room erupted in laughter and Jet winked at the President before continuing. "Excuse my jest, but when I heard that from an American friend, I just could not resist implementing your understanding of the current wave of anarchy that is sweeping America.

We, of course are funding all these groups and organizations along with our friend George Soros. I have been trying to figure out his game, but for the life of me I cannot understand his abject hatred for the country that made him a multibillionaire. It just doesn't compute but we welcome his assistance."

Jet smiled at the group and said, "We continue down the road with high hopes and great expectations but Comrades, in the final analysis our worst case scenario is about to play out. Don't know if you watched the debates, that everyone says Hillary won, but between you and me, she did not win. Trump won and he will win so we need to make our plans accordingly. I know I should not let a hint of defeat enter our deliberations but my head knows that we will have to deal with Donald Trump for the next four years and it will be difficult, very difficult and that is why our Zhanlue is so important. We will need to help all those in America that sign up to be Trump haters so that we can either shorten his reign, to something less than four years, or we make sure that he is not re-elected in 2020. It is a grave responsibility and one that we each must rededicate ourselves to win."

Jet sat down and thoughtful quiet settled in over the room. Finally, President Hu said, "Thank you, Jet for that sobering appraisal. Lin, what can you tell us about your inroads into the medical supply business?"

"Thank you Comrade. I have a confidential report for each of you that builds on the report you received at the last meeting. This new report has updated numbers and in every category, I repeat every category and sub group, we are making tremendous strides. I have no doubt that by the end of 2019 we will be far and away the world's leading manufacturer of all health care related products. It is a monumental undertaking but I have the cooperation of every medical source company in the country, and they are all eager to up their market share. In some cases, we have had to put more capital into some of the companies that we needed to acquire, but in all cases the investment will reap big dividends and so far we are operating within budget. The support staff has gone to almost 10,000 and there are now over 3000 companies that are engaged in upgrading their market share. I can say with confidence that come the end of 2019 we will be the dominate player in the world health care market and I predict that in some areas we will be close to the hundred percent level. In other words we will have captured the medical supply market and there will not be another country that is even close. If a medical disaster should strike the world, we can be assured that the Chinese people will have an uninterrupted supply of medical equipment and goods and that the rest of the world will be standing in line at the doors of our controlled facilities."

"Thank you comrade, your personal efforts and leadership do not go without notice by myself and your peers. Well Admiral, looks like you are last."

"Thank you Comrade President. Jet, I have had a team researching your suggestions about the Yellow River and the Bohai Sea area and initial tests show that the sediment in the bay may average over fifty meters. Everyone involved thinks it is a low cost solution to finding more productive land and we are proceeding with our investigation. Thank you again for your suggestion."

Jet gave the Admiral his best smile and nodded his thanks.

Continuing, the Admiral voiced his support for his team members and for the hundreds of professors around the national university system that were exploring hundreds of different options. "Before this program is over I think we will have a new awareness about our food supply and how it can work towards making us self-sufficient. It is truly a positive program that will serve us well for years to come."

With that said the Admiral seated himself and the President stood and thanked each participant for their dedication to the Zhanlue and then added, "In less than two weeks we will find out if Jet's predictions hold water. For once in my life I hope he is wrong but we must be prepared to face the future regardless of which way it goes. I urge all of you to make one last effort with all your American contacts to discourage their supporting Trump. I am thinking that it will be very, very close and this is truly the time that every vote will count. Thank you again for your participation and I shall look forward to seeing you all again after the new year. Jet will you join me in my office?"

With the goodbyes said, Jet and President Hu walked arm in arm to his office and when alone the President turned to his old friend and asked, "How is your wife doing?"

Jet's flashing eyes were quite and sad as he replied, "We hope to see the new year together, but that may not happen so right now it's just day-to-day."

"Take some time off and let this business go for a while. What happens from here on in is already well beyond our control and we will have plenty of time to react, whatever way the wind may blow. OK?"

"Yes, Yanlin, thank you."

CHAPTER
26

It was Wednesday morning in Beijing, November 9, and the newsroom had been reconfigured so that twelve people could comfortably view the proceedings. Twenty-four big screens surrounded the perimeter of the round room and the guests' seats were on a turntable that made the 360 degree circle every ten minutes. Each seat also rotated so the invited guest would not miss a minute of the circular action.

The President's select group included Jet and Hu's family members along with key ministers and of course the Vice Chairman and his family. Uniformed servers made sure each guest had his or her drink of preference and a never-ending supply of finger food was provided by the President's chef. It was eight a.m. and all eleven of the President's guests had found their assigned seats and every news channel in America was represented on the 24 screens.

Earlier at 7:05 p.m. eastern time the Associated Press called Indiana and Kentucky for Trump and Hillary was awarded Vermont which has voted Democratic in every election since 1988.

At 10:39 Ohio falls into the Trump camp and at 10:53 Florida also goes to Trump.

11:14 sees North Carolina called for Trump and at 11:56 Utah also goes for Trump. The Clinton camp now pins its fading hopes on getting Pennsylvania, Michigan and Wisconsin, but Pennsylvania goes to Trump at 1:35 and the nail in the coffin comes at 2:30 when Wisconsin puts Trump over the 270 threshold.

The President's guests had departed hours before the outcome was official but Jet and President Hu stayed until the bitter end.

"Well old friend, your intuition since day one was right on the money and I am still amazed that everyone in America got it wrong. How could they be so far off-base?"

Jet candidly replied, "They judge with their hopes and hearts, not their heads. That simple, Comrade."

"I guess you are right." The two men sat for several minutes watching the anchors dry their tears and close out their shows and finally President Hu asked, "Does the Russian collusion and disinformation campaign start today and do you think it will work?"

"Yes, it starts today and no, I don't think it will work. Oh it will be the main course that the American media feeds the people but Trump is tough. He will somehow weather the storm unless the Democrats can find something to pin on him that will lead to impeachment. I'm sure that Obama will order his democratic agency heads to pull all the stops on finding dirt and they may even be tempted to spy on him and his new people. Remember; Obama is still in power until the inauguration on January 20. That gives him," pausing Jet closed his eyes and calculated, "seventy-three days to pin the tail on the donkey, You can accomplish a lot in 73 days if all your agency heads are working hard to uncover dirt. They can wiretap Trump, they can make life difficult for the people he says he will appoint to pivotal positions and they can plant rumor after rumor that they were able to squeeze out of their Russian and Chinese friends."

President Hu laughed out loud and asked, "You really think that will all happen?"

"Comrade they already have a name for the covert operation to spy on Trump and his appointees during the transition. The operation is called 'Crossfire Hurricane' and all the agency heads, of all their intelligence agencies, are in on the plot." Looking with unusual intensity, even for Jet, at his President, Jet continued, "Comrade, this has never happened in American history, but it is happening now because they, the Washington democratic swamp dwellers, know that Trump cannot be bought, cannot be blackmailed and cannot be led and they will realize their power base is coming to a close. That of itself would be devastating but Trump also has to fight the old guard Republicans who like their power base and who have been living on the edge of the swamp for decades. So not only will he be fighting every Democrat but he will have his heels nipped by the Republican power base that is firmly entrenched in the Washington 'Good Old Boys Club'. So, smile my President, because every day for the next four years they, the swamp dwellers, will be making his life as miserable as they can and that, of course, means he will have little time to deal with us. When he does finally see us on his radar scope, we will do what we do best."

"And what old friend is that?"

"We listen carefully, we will agree that there are inequities, we state our willingness to change and we will, of course, ask for the needed time to study the problems so that we can find the solution that will best work for the interest of each country. We certainly cannot rush into any long-term agreement without adequate time to study all the possible solutions and their ramifications."

"You know Jet that in many circles you are depicted as a hatchet man, a diabolical and evil person and a ruthless adversity."

"Thank you Yanlin. I plead guilty on all counts and I have one more card to play."

"And what might that be?"

"It is rather long but I assume we have the time, and I am certain that you will appreciate the information, which I shall tie together in due course. One, the President-elect has indicated that General Flynn will be his national security adviser. I met the General several years ago at a conference in Germany and he is all business and he knows, since he worked for Obama, where all the bodies are buried and believe me, Mr. Obama was in charge of the mortuary. I don't think Obama and the intelligence agency heads will allow the General access to bring their secrets to the light of day and therefore I look for them to sabotage the General in any way possible. In the process the General, to save his own hide, might be tempted to make up lies about Trump. Such as, Trump and Putin have a secret relationship, Trump and Putin worked together to steal the election from Hillary, Trump and Putin had the same mistress in Moscow and on and on. We, of course, with the Sterling report and with leaks by Ambassador Qiliang are currently trying to plant these negatives throughout the American government and some of them may turn out to be the key to impeachment. At any rate, we shall keep the rumor mill churning and hope that some of it sticks to teflon Trump. Two, there is a situation brewing in Ukraine all wrapped up with Biden's son, the one we gave the five-billion dollar contract to, that may come around to bite Mr. Trump and we will continue working with contacts like George Soros to lay that trap. Three, if all else fails and in late 2019 Trump is coasting along and looks like he will win re-election, we will spring the Dragons breath trap, which I don't think he will be able to survive. By that time we will have unchallenged control over the medical supply business and shortages of medical supplies, during a pandemic, will be the last nail in his coffin. So you see my President, we have a full arsenal and every day for the next four years we and the willing allies in the mainstream American media will be shooting bullets at Mr. Trump. He can't dodge them all."

"You have me convinced. I will definitely sleep better tonight. Thank you for refreshing my understanding and thank you Jet for your loyalty to our cause. You are truly a national treasure and I just may have your brain housed in the National Museum."

CHAPTER 27

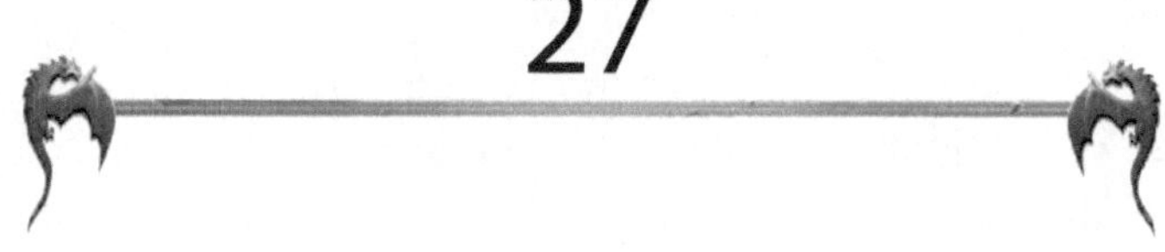

February 28, Chinese New Year, the year of the Rooster, was traditional and President Hu loved every minute of the pomp and circumstance. The ball room capacity was 8,000 and every seat was occupied by a Chinese citizen that was somehow connected to the higher echelon of the Peoples Republic. They were all special and they all enjoyed privileges and perks that the average Chinese, one of 1.379 billion, could not even dream of obtaining. Since 1949 when Chiang Kai-shek fled to Taiwan to escape Mao Xedong and his Communist followers the beneficiaries of the system were the children of the elite thug-like loyal party members. No one rose through the ranks of the army or any of the civilian agencies without some form of nepotism rearing its ugly head. As a result, nescience was a given and foot dancing ones way into leadership positions, with children in tow, was just part of the drill. It made for a bureaucracy that was slow, sluggish, slave to the status quo and of course narcissistic.

President Hu knew that the system was rigged but it was so deeply entrenched that any thought of a merit based change was totally out of the question. The creature was just to massive to move or change so the top tier just smiled at the underlings and if someone obtained leadership that was out of proportion to their capabilities they could be judged an enemy of the state and simply disappear along with their family and in some extreme cases even their friends. This realization, by the rank and file and those 8,000, at today's special new year event, meant that everyone was guarded. You carefully chose those to mingle with, those to share political ideas with and even then most were always looking over their shoulders, wondering if they had been overheard or misunderstood. It was truly a caste system, but unlike some caste systems, where you can tell the rank by outward appearance, there was no way to know who might be the watched or the watcher. Nerve-racking to be sure but just part of life under communist rule for the last, almost fifty years.

Karl Marx, Vladimir Lenin, and Joseph Stalin had no idea that their suggested system could be taken so far. Far beyond the Russian-based original that had relied on just normal human fears to a fear-based society where you, as parents, might be turned in by the very children you had worked so hard to push up the ladder.

Jet How was not at his leader's side as his wife had made it to see new years but the prognosis was for only a few more days and Jet was staying near home to console the children and the rest of the extended family that made a living pressing his coat tails. He saw it, and it concerned him, but he chose to ignore the obvious as it was too ingrained. Too much a part of the government and the life he and his peers had carved out of the Chinese countryside. He had used the system as his father had been one of Mao's favorite Generals.

Smiling to himself and thinking about the past years and the system he had helped build he was proud but at the same time knew that millions of his countrymen lived lives of fear and hardship. Millions existing on what the average American spends on coffee each day with no glimmer of freedom from their entrapment. Jet had seen the difference when he traveled to Hong Kong. The same base, the same lineage, the same ancestors, yet the people of Hong Kong were different. Freedom, learned under British rule, had made the difference, given them a sense of pride in personal achievement and few were fearful of the government. They were bold and bright, eager to try new ideas and not willing to be controlled by anyone, not ever the Communist party.

Sadly, he thought, 'The day will come, and soon, when we will have to either put Hong Kong under our thumb or face the possibility of losing the whole country and fifty years of hard work. How can you let Hong Kong remain free and deny that same freedom to 1.379 billion of their fellow countrymen?' He almost laughed when he further thought, 'Anyway there aren't that many bullets.'

The New Year celebration was capped the next morning with a massive military parade that surpassed by tenfold what the little troll in Pyongyang trotted out every year. It was mind numbing for the President to realize that all those soldiers were there to invoke his will and that he was, in fact, their absolute master. On the reviewing stand he was flanked by thousands and thousands of loyal comrades, and they all bowed to his every whim and desire, as if he was a god, sent down from paradise to lead these mindless robots. It occurred to the President, watching his troops go by that his position should not be one arbitrary established by forced term limits but rather should be a lifetime position. The idea totally sucked up his brain and every fiber of his being shouted, "YES". He smiled and started planning the conversation that he would have with Jet next week. After all Jet, of all the people in the world, would understand and that magnificent brain would find a way for the President to realize his newfound dream, President for life.

Looking around at his kingdom he realized what a glorious day it was to make such a history-bending decision.

CHAPTER
28

As President Hu sat on his patio, deep within his secure bunker, he could not help smiling. In fact, he had been smiling ever since the year of the Rooster was ushered into the history books and he had made the decision to become China's first lifetime leader. Even the great Mao Zedong had not been able to make that bird fly.

It was already the middle of March and while the President's wheels had been turning, in his quest to be the lifetime President, not one of the other 1.3 billion Chinese had even considered the question.

Jet's arrival was communicated by a series of chime sounds that did not intrude on the serenity of the garden. Yanlin looked up from the documents he was studying and was pleased to see Jet emerging from the office and striding his way. The President thought, 'for a man his age he still moves well, hope my genes are as strong.'

"Jet, old friend so good to see you and I was distressed when I heard that your wife had passed. How are you doing?"

"Well it wasn't a surprise, but it is still difficult to comprehend, but that is life and all we can do as survivors is continue down our path. Don't you agree Yanlin?"

"Of course. Come sit and tell me where you have been and what dragons you have slain."

Jet smiled, lowered himself into an upholstered wicker chair, opposite the President and exhaled deeply, looked around and exclaimed, "I envy you this place. It is so relaxing. It's like a velvet glove encasing your body and whisking away all the problems of the real world. Yes, my President, you have created paradise and when I am gone you can dump my ashes at the top of the waterfall so I can forever enjoy your world."

"Well we certainly are in a melancholy mood today and that may help you solve a problem that has been cluttering up my mind since New Years."

Before Jet could react, the President launched into his dilemma by asking, "Jet, do you know the word oligarchy?"

Jet looked deep into his brain, came up with a glimmer, but replied in a slow thoughtful cadence, "No, Yanlin - I - don't - but - I am thinking - that it may be a form of government where all authority is in the hands of a few."

"Exactly" the President almost shouted, "Exactly and if you look around and think honest thoughts you would have to agree that our current system is indeed an oligarchy. Yes, we have the NPC (National People's Congress), the State Council members which includes me, five State Councilors, the Secretary General and 26 ministers and then there is the CMC (Central Military Commission) which I head and carry the title of Commander-in- Chief."

Jet, looking at his long-time leader asked, "Where are you going with this civic lesson my President?"

"Of course, cut to the chase, no lead-up required is your middle name, so I will tell you where this is going; you are going to figure out how I am to become President for LIFE !. Jet was not surprised, not in the least, in fact he had been expecting the question for some time and he full well understood how the new year's events, the magnitude of the parade and all the bowing and scrapping could affect the President and his inner most thoughts.

"To tell you the truth Yanlin, I have been expecting this question for some time and I think it is perfectly natural that you would aspire to the ultimate position. So, you want our government to change from an oligarchy to a monarchy. By the way the definition of a monarchy is undivided sovereignty or rule of a single person."

Looking at Jet, the only man in the world with which he could share such ambition, the President said nothing, just nodded his head and smiled.

Jet leaned back, closed his eyes and said, "Comrade President I think you are already there, and I think that with a few late night private dinners and some gentle persuasion a vote can be taken, at the next NPC meeting, that will accomplish your goal. I will work up a list of those that will need to be enlightened and then at the next session the measure can be introduced and voted into law. After all, everyone, even NPC members, know that even important people and their families can simply vanish. Its just part of life."

President Yanlin looked across the table at his old friend, eyes closed, head back, totally relaxed and thought, 'I am certainly glad he is on my side as he may just have enough power to make me disappear, if he so wished.'

CHAPTER
29

General Long had been addressing the Group of five for almost thirty minutes and his level of commitment to the pacification program was inspiring. Even Jet was caught up in the problem, process and the solutions that the General was setting forth.

"In summary, Comrades, this exercise will give us real hands-on experience and will pinpoint any modifications that may be required to make our plan totally workable. Questions?"

President Hu asked, "So the invasion will take place on April 18 and finish two weeks later. What would be the best time for me to visit?"

The General didn't hesitate, just scanned his notes and said, "I have you penciled in for Friday April 28, if that can be arranged."

President Hu looked at Jet and asked, "Can you accompany me Comrade?"

"Of course, I shall look forward to the cool mountains, as I understand Spring does not come to that region until mid to late May."

"Then it is settled. Thank you General. We shall be looking forward to seeing your pacification plans up close." Pausing the President turned to Jet and asked, "Is there a African or South American county that is floundering, on the verge of autarchy, that might possibly endanger our national security and therefore would need to take advantage of the General's newly developed skills?"

Jet smiled at his leader and quipped, "Sounds like a question I should have asked comrade." Then quickly continuing he stated, "Yes, there are some hotspots and I will have a recommendation for you within the week." With a twinkling smile he added, "Closer to home, might you consider our stout friend in Pyongyang as a prime target? The rest of the world would, I am sure, applaud our efforts to return him to a non-nuclear power, agrarian monarch."

"Now Jet, how can you talk about my favorite ally like that?" Then with an evil grin he continued, "But it certainly would be an interesting exercise. After all, it's not like Chinese troops have never been across the Yalu River."

Jet looked off in space remembering the difficult decision it was to send Chinese troops directly into combat against the American army in October 1950. He had a hand in planning the operation and his eldest son was one of the 180,000 Chinese that were killed in North Korea. His son's body was never recovered as well as over seven thousand American troops that are still classified as missing in action.

"Jet," He hears his name and coming back from his brief trip into the past he replied, "Yes, yes, I hear you. I was just lost in the past for a minute comrades. Please excuse this old man's remembrances."

"No problem comrade, I too remember that your son was lost in Korea. So back to reality. General, we will not be putting Korea on top of your list."

The group around the table all smiled and Lin Wong asked, "Is it time for my report Comrade President?"

"By all means, Lin."

"I have to be frank comrades, when I started this undertaking, I did not realize that it would cover so much ground in such a short time. As of today, I think we have maxed out in that we have over 4,500 companies chasing the medical supply train. There are thousands of individual items in that medical supply chain and in each sub-grouping we are striving for one-hundred percent coverage. In other words, please visualize a large metropolitan hospital and then consider every item they use, on a daily basis, from band aids to the most sophisticated x-ray and scanning machines and you will get an idea of the scope of this project. The booklet in front of you is divided into sections like, Clinic Equipment, Equipment, Compression Therapy and Hosiery, Pharmaceuticals and Sundries and so on and so forth. Under each heading we list the Chinese companies that are pursuing each individual item in each sub-grouping and the figures in red are the percentage of coverage a year ago, the blue numbers are current coverage percentages and the green numbers represent our projected coverage by the end of 2019.

There is not an individual item that has not gone up and as you can see, in some cases we are nearing the 90% mark of world market share. A recent U.S. News report said the following, 'State-owned Chinese companies, buoyed by heavy government subsidies, set their prices so low that they are able to undercut established manufacturers in the U.S. and elsewhere, prompting them to shut down their plants and move their operations to China.' Questions?"

"Thank you Lin, and last but not least, what do you have for us Admiral Wanguan on the food expansion front?"

"Well Comrade President, I am pleased to report that the marginal land search, that is lands currently not being utilized for any kind of food production, has reached over a million hectares. In other words, we have identified non-productive land and now have teams looking at what kind of products we can grow on these lands depending on soil, water and weather conditions. It is a challenging research project but every University is contributing time and talent to come up with new products and procedures to maximize the output of each hectare. In the rice growing areas we are looking at mechanical planting, weeding and harvesting machinery, but it is somewhat of a double-edged sword."

"How so?" Jet asked.

"I will give you an example. In Northern California the rice seed is flown onto flooded fields. One crop seeding plane can do thousands of hectares per day, whereas we may put a hundred people on a 90 hectare field and it will take a week of backbreaking labor to plant the seedlings. There is all manner of logistics that enter the mix in that the rice seedlings, planted by hand, keep growing every day and soon they are too large to plant in that the roots intertwine and get damaged during separation, prior to planting. If we were to reconfigure the current rice land into thousand hectare plots, rather than small terraced fields, and fly the seeds onto the manpower requirement would be drastically impacted. All the best brains in the agriculture field know about the mechanical planters and harvesters, used in places like Northern California, but none are suggesting we go that route as it would mean millions of rice farmers would be unemployed and would migrate to cities to find work, so they could feed their families. China is unique and under our current system we produced over 250 million tons of rice whereas in Northern California they will produce less than 10 million tons. We shall continue to research our biggest crop but for now we are not recommending any changes, other than possibly converting some of the marginal lands into rice producing areas. Questions?"

"No questions?, well Comrades that brings us to a very sensitive point in our discussions. Jet and I and just a handful of people are privileged to the information you are about to receive." Looking steel black daggers around the table he continued by saying, "Comrades the information I share with you today can never go beyond this room. None of you will discuss the subject among yourselves or with any other person, on the pain of death for you and all you may know or love. As of yesterday, we have over 4 million Dragon Breath delivery systems situated around the world. In every country, in every world port the systems are charged and ready to dispense. The trigger, that releases the Dragon Breath, is controlled by the Army and their satellite defense system and can only be activated on my personal orders. We hope that Mr. Trump will not push us and will stay so busy, keeping the wolves from his heels, that China will fall beneath the radar. But should our efforts to cut short his term in office fails and we project that he might win the 2020 election, we will not hesitate to release the Dragon Breath on America and for that matter the entire world. Do not be concerned for your personal health as at your next scheduled physical you will receive a vaccination that will make you immuned. Special clinics will be set up to vaccinate your family and friends and eventually everyone in government and in company leadership positions will also be vaccinated. As we increase serum output, the Army and all its people will also be covered and eventually every man, woman and child in China will be covered. Thank you for your attention and have a pleasant trip home. We will schedule the next meeting after the exercise in Tibet."

Other than Jet, the participants around the table were wide eyed, sober and all business as they departed with more information that any of them ever wanted to have and it would be a weight they would carry the rest of their lives. When the room was clear, President Hu said, "Jet, please look into the Hong Kong situation for me."

"What do you have in mind?"

"General Long's plan may very well be the horse we need to bring Hong Kong back into line. After all the British have been gone since July 1, 1997, what's that?"

Jet piped in, "Almost 20 years."

"Yes, twenty years and the agreement is good through 2047, so if we up the timeframe and cancel 'the one country, two system relationship' what the hell are the British, or for that matter, the rest of the world going to do? Call us names and make threats are their only options and we can certainly weather that storm."

"So what you are saying is that after the Tibet exercise we unleash the General and his army on Hong Kong and put an end to the one country, two system relationship, now, rather than waiting for 2047?"

"Correct, and when we are in Tibet, I want you to schedule a one-on-one meeting with the General, tell him what we are planning and ask him to put together a complete plan for the pacification and return of Hong Kong into the system that lets us control the rest of the country."

Jet looked at his leader and asked, looking up at the ceiling for guidance from his ancestral gods, "And you accuse me of hatching diabolical schemes."

"Are you suggesting that we may be ancestral twins?"

"Yes, and this twin is hungry!"

"Will lunch on the patio be acceptable, brother?"

CHAPTER
30

The flight rules into Nyingchi Maining Airport, at 9,834 feet above sea level, required RNP or Required Navigation Performance which was no big deal for the presidential jet in that Boeing 757's regularly plied the route from the country's largest airport at Lhasa Gongga.

The approach up the Tsango River valley was interesting in that at the narrowest point, the distance between the mountain peaks, was only 4 km. Jet smiled as he thought of the airport in Queenstown, New Zealand, remembering that there too you look up at the mountains on final approach.

Jet and President Hu, and the staffs, were awed by the majestic beauty of their surroundings as they made the final approach looking up at snow covered peaks on either side. Both men could recall that in 1950 China had to invade Tibet to reclaim the territory that they had lost in 1913, when Tibet had broken away from their Chinese masters. Since then India and China had almost been on a full-blown war footing arguing about the international borders. In fact, two of the nearby counties of Medog and Zayui were currently under dispute and about half of each county was ruled by China and the other half by the Arunachal Pradesh District of India.

General Long would have to tread lightly as the influx of the Chinese Army, this close to the border, was a red flag for the bulls of India. In fact, the General had notified the Indian Government, through their Embassy in New Delhi, that the Chinese government was conducting exercises from mid-April to May 5, in the Ningchi boarder region and that India should not be concerned about the unusual amount of Chinese Army activity in the area.

At landing time, the temperature was 16c or almost 61f and the mild cloudless sky was a welcome respite from the hot humidity of Beijing.

As President Hu stepped onto Tibetan soil, he was the first Chinese President to do so. The Peoples Republic, in 1950, had negotiated a Seventeen Point Agreement with the newly enthroned 14th Dalai Lama that stayed valid until 1959, the year of the Tibetan Rebellion. Those years, known in China as the Great Leap Forward, may have caused the deaths of between 200,000 and 1 million Tibetans. Over 6,000 monasteries were destroyed and as a result the vast majority of Tibetan architecture and historical artifacts were lost. In 1962 China and India fought over the borders and China won the conflict but withdrew north, effectively ceding the Arunachal Pradesh district to India.

President Hu was greeted by General Long, the ranking commander and hundreds of government administrators. The line of silent greeters were a mix of Chinese and Tibetan ethnicity but they all had one thing in common and that was their silent, almost reverent respect for their supreme leader.

At the end of the receiving line the President's motorcade was waiting and he and Jet and their staffs were transported to the city center and the cities best four star hotel, The Chongquing Cygnet. The Executive Suite had been reserved for the President and Jet and the staffs were divided up between fourteen deluxe suites.

The evening's banquet was a mixture of Chinese and Tibetan pomp and circumstance, and President Hu could see that the General was enjoying the presentation almost as much as he was. The brightly clothed participant put on a lively show that was greeted with much enthusiasm by locals and visitors alike. During the course of the evening the General informed the President that India had brought up several battalions to counter the presence of the large Chinese troop contingent on their contested border.

The next morning at breakfast, President Hu and Jet received a briefing from General Long. The President opened the session by asking, "How many troops are participating in this exercise General?"

"Just over fifteen thousand. They are at every main intersection through the city, and throughout the inhabited areas. The city has a population of about 60 thousand and there are another 40 thousand or so in the nearby counties. We have restricted all movement without permits and all utilities and transportation links are controlled by our personnel. Over fifty percent of our men have a good understanding of the local language so we are not having any communication problems. Ten days ago we evacuated all the tourists from the area and plane, train, bus, and automobile traffic has been curtailed to emergency only needs.

We have a bit of a problem as some of the local leaders seem to think this is a permament change and I am having trouble convincing them otherwise. If you have a chance, you may dispel their concerns if you could confirm that all of our troops will be out of the area no later than May 5, at which time business as usual can be reinstated."

"Of course General and what is on the agenda for today?"

"We shall visit the different government entities that control the water, electricity, transportation and several of the larger distribution centers that specialize in moving food in and out of the area. All of these areas are being operated and controlled by army personnel; however, the civilian counterparts are on the job as well to provide support and training. Overall, I can see that the matrix for this operation can be applied to any place or region of our choice."

"Well General, I am impressed with how you pulled this off and in such a short time. I have just one question, however, before asking, you must understand that your next exercise will be deadly serious and I will expect that you will lose personnel and that the other side will lose as well, so it rises well above the level of war games or a mere exercise."

The General was taken back and silently waited for this commander in chief to continue.

"General, please have all your people clear the room so that the three of us can continue." nodding toward Jet.

"Of course Comrade."

The word was passed down the chain and within minutes the room was occupied by only President Hu, Jet and General Long.

"General there is unrest in Hong Kong. Some of the new regulations that we have quietly been imposing are meeting with stiff resistance and as we come closer to eliminating the 'one country, two system' relationship it will only get more difficult. I am convinced that we must act sooner, than later and Hong Kong's special status must be revoked. We cannot have one city, out of the thousands in our country, operating under a different set of rules. It breeds discontent and anarchy and I will not stand for either. Please draw up plans, on a critical timeframe schedule, for the pacification of Hong Kong. I would like to see the plan on my desk by the end of July. If you need to wrap up this operation early, then by all means do so, but have the plan ready by July 31. You can use Jet to help you get through and around the politics of this maneuver. Questions?"

"No Comrade, I fully understand the seriousness of this assignment and I look forward, over the next week, to getting up to speed on the exact details of the Hong Kong problem and look forward to working with Comrade Jet. I am going to leave my second in command, General Zhang Youxia to finish out this operation as I would like to depart this morning for my base. I only have seventy days to develop the plan and I assume I will need every single day."

The General wondered if he had just stepped in it and as a way to make his departure more palatable, he said, "I had planned to take you to the Buchu Monastery and the Xiuba Ancient Castle, from the 4th century, but maybe you would rather do that another time?"

"No, I think I would enjoy that today and if General Youxia is available I will look forward to having him as our escort."

"That can be arranged. Excuse me, I shall return shortly with the General."

General Long hurried out of the breakfast room, found General Youxia waiting at the door, took him aside and said in quick military cadence, "You are in charge of this operation. I must immediately return to the base for a new, highly classified assignment just given me by the President. Come with me and be prepared to follow today's established schedule. By the way you can wrap up this operation any time you are ready, prior to the original May 5 cutoff, if you like. Questions?"

"No Sir, understood."

Good to his word General Long was back in seconds with General Youxia in tow. "Comrade President may I present my second in command, General Zhang Youxia"

President Hu shook hands with his new escort and introduced him to Jet by saying, "General, you need to meet my eyes and ears, Comrade Jet How Chung."

The men shook hands and Jet matter of factly said, "General, I am sure you have other important duties but we appreciate your being our escort for the rest of the day. It will give us all a chance to get acquainted and I want you to know that the rumors about my eating young children and having my way with the palace virgins are categorically not true."

The four men laughed, General Long said his farewells and General Youxia stated, " We can depart from the front entrance in one hour, if that is agreeable with you Comrade President."

"Fine General, see you then." Jet replied.

The Buchu Monastery was just 28km from the hotel and the ride went quickly. The scenery was grand and the open air car, while a bit breezy, afforded unparalleled views of the towering snow-covered mountains. Mount Everest was only 700 km. away and the feeling of being on the roof of the world was easily understood. Miles from the monastery, the road afforded glimpses of the white monastery building with its golden roof, as it was situated near the top of a rounded hill. The tour of the building was conducted by all eight of the monks who made the monastery their permanent home and the artwork while interesting, was crude when compared to the ancient works found in the Chinese museums.

The second stop on the tour was to be a 4th century castle, now in ruins and Lake baksumtso, but when President Hu found out it was an additional 122 km. he decided to forego the trip. Jet was pleased, the General was pleased and the ride back to Nyingchi was cool, relaxing and pleasant. Near noon the motorcade was passing near the Lulang forest which is a vast alpine setting where the forest is made up of picea, asperata and pinewood trees with meadows of tall grass and spring flowers in abundance. Stopping at a small roadside village the President, Jet and the General treated themselves to an outdoor lunch, while the ever present security detail tried to remain invisible. The general recommended tsampa which is the staple food of Tibet. Tsampa is a flour milled from roasted barley made into a bun. It is then filled with meat and cabbage and served with small bowls of Yak butter tea, followed by chang, a beer-like drink made from kodo millet or rice. It was a pleasant interlude and Jet was taking an immediate liking to General Youxia as the younger man had a quick wit and did not seem the least bit intimidated by his present company.

As they neared the hotel in downtown Bayi, Jet asked, "What time does the meeting with the local government heads start?"

The General answered with a big smile, "Assembly at five, dinner at six and then you can leave early tomorrow morning for your trip home. I understand that the local government leaders are looking forward to bending your ears with lists of needs, but I can curtail that if you wish."

"No", the President replied, "Let them have their say. Much can be learned about leaders when you listen to their 'want lists', much of which I find to be personal rather than what might help the people. I will give you a wink General when I have had enough."

"As you wish, Comrade."

The banquet, low key yet up to presidential guest status was relaxing and enjoyable and you could tell that the local dignitaries had not a clue what had been going on in their backyard for the past two weeks. To many, in the beginning, it had seemed like a true military takeover yet there was no reason. There were few dissenters in the area as over the last fifty plus years the iron hand of Chinese communism had ruled. The local government heads were loyal to their masters and if any area in the world had ever been pacified it was current-day Tibet. Heads were still being scratched as to the purpose of the quasi-invasion and no answers were forthcoming from the visiting dignitaries.

President Hu did make a brief speech where he thanked the people of Tibet for their hospitality and finished by saying that the insights that the Army had gained from their interaction with the local government officials had been valuable and they, the People's Republic, sincerely appreciated the cooperation that the Tibetans had exhibited. Closing he announced that the sum of 100 million yuan or RMB (Ren Min Bi) as the Tibetans referred to the yuan, would be coming their way to upgrade infrastructure and transportation. The announcement met with polite applause but still did not answer the question as to what the military exercise was all about.

Years later, as China gobbled up South American and African countries, in their quest for world dominance, did the astute remember the Tibet exercise, and were able to put two and two together.

The flight back to Beijing was uneventful and Jet and President Hu congratulated themselves and looked forward to equal success in the upcoming pacification of Hong Kong. Neither was looking forward to the confrontation as they both knew it would be a bloody affair before the final curtain fell.

CHAPTER
31

As Jet made his way to the President's office, in the underground bunker, he shook his head wondering where the time had gone. Seemed like only yesterday he and Yanlin were flashing over Southeastern Tibet on their way back home, and here it was July 31 already and time for decision making on Hong Kong.

The elder statesman had no illusions that this was going to be one tough nut to crack but in the end, he knew that the might of the state would win out. Hong Kong must be moved from their status as Asia's quasi-financial center to just another Chinese city, no more, no less.

Jet wondered if General Long had the guts to ramrod the operation or if he would bend. 'If I were a betting man, I would bet he caves before the job is completed, after all we are talking about just over 7 million people that have tasted freedom for the last 50 years and it is going to be one difficult sale.'

Jet arrived at the conference room first and seated himself in his usual place, leaned back, closed his eyes and reviewed the action plan he had developed if the General's plan fell short. General Long and Yanlin arrived a few minutes before nine and the General's demur told Jet that here was a man that might be outside his element.

"Good morning Comrades," was the President's opening and both men bowed to their leader and repeated the greeting and reseated themselves. The General had three notebooks in front of him and carefully slid them across the table to Jet and President Hu.

"Well General, we will be interested to see what you have planned to solve our dilemma."

"Thank you Comrade President. I think it is a bold plan that will let the state bring Hong Kong back into line with all other city and county governments. Jet has shown me the rules and regulations that have been developed and everyone involved agrees that we can expect demonstrations when these rules are published to the general public. I suggest that the first demonstrations be met with extremely harsh treatment and that the Navy takes the lead. We will deploy to Hong Kong harbor, prior to enactment of the regulations, two aircraft carriers with forty heavy lift helicopters. Six large landing craft ships, the kind that can run right up on the beach, 300 smaller landing craft and a force of 20 thousand marines which will be housed on their ships in the harbor. Each carrier will have 20 platforms, 10 by 10 meters square that can accommodate 625 men and their riot equipment. For example, if the demonstrators set up in Kowloon near the airport we will airlift in the troops and will face them down. If they do not cease their demonstrations the troops will fire on them and keep firing until they are neutralized. The wounded and killed will be loaded on the platforms, taken twenty miles offshore and dumped."

"Those arrested will be taken to the nearest landing craft, loaded and taken to their final destination which is Sal Kung East County Park. It is a nearby island location and we shall turn the entire island into a prison camp. Hospital tents will be erected all over the island to house the protesters until they can be brought to trial or until they sign fingerprinted forms that they will never again engage in protest demonstrations, upon pain of death for the perpetrator and their extended families. The small landing craft will be used to transfer our personnel between ships and the prison island and to transport small groups of protesters from any of the surrounding areas. Each protester released will be tattooed on the back of their right hand. Anyone re-arrested with a tattoo will automatically be executed."

"And that Comrades is the guts of the plan and all equipment and all personnel will be ready for action by year-end, upon your approval."

Jet looked at General and commented, "I think it is brilliant to let the navy and the marines do the dirty work. That way the Hong Kong police will not forever be hated by the surviving citizens. I also like the fact that from your ships in mid-harbor you can move quickly to any location, be it on Hong Kong island itself, the new territories or the Kowloon side. Yes, I like it. Job well done, General."

"Thank you comrade."

President Hu looked up from his notebook and calmly said, "General, take the necessary steps to implement your plans so that you will be ready to move any time after new year. I think it would be well for us to have a meeting with Admiral Xi Jinping in the near future and I will take care of making those arrangements and will shortly notify you when and where."

"Unless you or Jet have something else, I think we can close this meeting. Thank you for your service to your country and have a pleasant trip back to your base."

General Long nodded to his superiors and departed leaving Jet and President Hu smiling at each other.

Jet broke the silence, "You certainly know how to pick them Comrade. I didn't think the General would rise to the occasion, so I am pleasantly surprised."

"Let's have lunch." the President replied, "I'm hungry.!"

CHAPTER
32

The first state visit of Donald Trump to China took place in early November 2017 and was hailed by the administration as historic; however, the indictments of Paul Manafort and Rick Gates by the Mueller Probe, on November fourth, weighed heavily on the President and his men.

Jet, who was never far from President Hu's side had spent millions getting the Democratic machine, the Sterling Report and the Mueller probe up and running and was almost certain that the Russian collusion story would spell an end to the Trump reign. He enjoyed smiling at his blond haired adversary and interrupting his words for the President, putting his spin on the comments, in the process, was just part of the game.

The two leaders agreed early that their Sino-US relationship and ties would be at the head-of-state level rather than pushing the work down the chain. Jet tried to discourage the arrangement but the two Presidents were in early agreement that they needed to be heavily invested in the process.

The three-day schedule included focus on iconic Chinese culture, visits to the Palace Museum, watching the Peking Opera, touring the Forbidden City and various other welcoming ceremonies and state dinners.

In their private talks, where just the two Presidents and Jet was the only people in the room, Mr. Trump minced no words about the trade imbalance and was blunt, that if necessary, he would impose heavy tariffs to help balance the relationship. Jet, a student of body language and physiology knew that he was watching one confident man that would not hesitate to call a spade, a spade and would do what others might just threaten.

The US President focused on his resolve to denuclearize North Korea, promoting a free and open Indo-Pacific region and advancing American prosperity through fair and reciprocal trade, and if the latter required, tariffs that would be his weapon of choice.

Before landing in China, the President had stopped in Hawaii to thank the American military and pay his respects at Pearl Harbor. From there he winged into Japan where he met the Emperor Akihito and Empress Michiko, Prime Minister Shinzo Abe and reaffirmed America's unshakable alliance with Japan as they both faced the North Korean nuclear threat.

In South Korea the meetings with President Moon Jae-in were cordial and productive and at Camp Humphrey, near the DMZ he thanked American and South Korean troops. The trip finished up with visits to Vietnam and the Philippines. In Da Nang he delivered an address to the APEC CEO summit again outlining his vision of an open Indo-Pacifc region where free, fair and reciprocal trade was the center piece of all relationships.

As Jet and President Hu were reviewing the visit it was obvious to both men that eight years of Trump would not, be in China's long-term interest. Sitting by the fire, in the President's office on a cold and chilly late November evening, Jet declared, "Yanlin, based on what I see Mr. Trump rises to the level of an archenemy. In other words, our biggest protagonist and our worst enemy."

The words hung heavy as both men stared into the fire. Finally, President Hu stood up, stretched, yawned and announced, "Then we will just have to let the dragon breathe on him."

CHAPTER
33

During President Trump's trip to China, when he had his one on one with President Hu and Jet How Chung it was obvious that the very real threat of tariffs was Mr. Trump's biggest stick. As Jet and the President discussed the subject, near year-end, Jet asked, "Do you remember when we talked about this last year I recommended that we listen carefully, nod our understanding and agreement and then take time to make changes, well here we are."

"How so?"

"Look, we know his solution and some selective tariffs are not going to break the bank so we give in. We also agree to buy more American wheat, grain and all the other farm products that are on the list. We agree to stop acquiring intellectual properties on the side, in fact we let him win on almost every point and we sign an agreement to seal the deal."

"I am sorry old friend but you have lost me. How is agreeing on every point they raise in our best interests?"

"Because, buried deep in the agreement, on say page 2,500, we put in a clause, with flowery language, that will be difficult to translate. The clause will say, 'In the case of a worldwide crisis, something as serious as a pandemic or a major worldwide war, this agreement is null and void.'"

Jet smiled at his leader, settled deeper into the leather couch, and waited for a reaction.

Almost five minutes went by before the supreme leader of the People's Republic ventured a comment. "So Mr. China, if I understand you the plan is to have big delegation meetings in Washington and in China. Send hundreds of trade representatives from every segment of our economy who will meet with their American counterparts. Give and take and give and take and make each meeting a big political show of reconciliation, at the highest level. Schedule the talks to run almost a full year because the subject is so big and has so many elements. Along the way send the Vice Premier to Washington for serious high level talks and invite the Vice President, Mr. Pence, to China for final high level negotiations. Then, to cap it off I will go to Washington for signing of the historical agreement. Mr. Trump will have months of positive press, he will be euphoric about what great friends we are and buried in the agreement on page 2,500, will be the kicker. We will have eaten up another year of his presidency and it will be near the time that we shall be forced to let the Tiger out of his den. We will let the virus loose in the Wuhan area, making sure that it is sealed off from China but wide open to international travel. We will urge, with a capital U, Wuhan citizens to travel the world but will restrict their travel in China. The pandemic will spread like wildfire, Mr. Trump will be unable to control the outbreak because we shall, by that time, control the worldwide medical supply chain. All during 2020, right up to election night, he will be fighting the devastating impact of the virus. His economy will be in the tank. There will be massive layoffs and unemployment will soar to record levels and then BLM (Burn, Loot and Murder) will be turned loose on the streets and chaos will follow. Makes no difference who the democrats run Trump will lose and we will be rid of him and maybe a million of his fellow citizens." Smiling from ear-to-ear as he paced in front of the fire the People's President announced, "If we are lucky, Mr. Biden will be his replacement and we know from past experience that controlling him is easy, it only takes money."

The President flopped down on the couch, next to Jet and said, "You and your ideas certainly can make a man thirsty. Let's have a bottle of that Sake of yours to celebrate."

Jet How nodded agreement, leaned back, closed his eyes and thought, "I could have been the supreme leader, IF....."

CHAPTER
34 (Part A)

The e-mail message from Lin Lee invoked the 'Tiger' prefix and used semi-coded language to outline the emergency.

"Tiger- Organization that was top of my list has new finance head. She, Susan Rosenberg, advises our leadership positions will disappear unless we meet funding requirement by month end. Cannot think of 50 million reason to continue. Could we meet soon?"

Jet, read and reread and instantly knew that BLM was shaking them down for 50 million dollars. Who was this Susan Rosenberg? He immediately dialed his communication chief and opened the conversation with, "I am only going to say this once. By 5 p.m. I want every spec of data you can find on the American organization call Black Lives Matter. Names of key employees, headquarter locations, history and also on a woman name Susan Rosenberg that works for BLM parent company called Thousand Currents. Get me everything. Got it Feng?"

Jet didn't wait for the communications director to answer, but switched off his phone, sat down at his desk, activated his desk top computer and began searching google, for himself.

Two hours later, with a stack of printed out fact sheets Jet sat down in front of the fireplace, kicked off his shoes and commenced to read the data he had gathered.

'So', he thought, 'Looks like Thousand Currents, is a 501(c)(3) nonprofit and is the fiscal sponsor of BLM. So what's a nonprofit 501?

Reading on he found out. 'To be tax-exempt under section 501(c)(3) of the Internal Revenue Code, an organization must be organized and operated exclusively for exempt purposes set forth in section 501(c)(3) and none of its earnings may inure to any private shareholder or individual.' 'So what's inure mean?' 'Best I can figure is benefit but the word accustom is used as well and that means to make familiar with something through use or experience, so earnings cannot benefit the parties, bet there are ways around that Sherlock.'

'So who runs Thousand Currents? Here it is: For almost 35 years Thousand Currents, (formerly IDEX) has invested more than US$10 million in 1,000 community-led initiatives in the Global South. Today we are exchanging grassroots brilliance for lasting and transformative change. Our partners are currently working with and connected to over 200 million women, small farmers, indigenous peoples, urban residents, sexual and ethnic minorities and youth. We continue to stand in solidarity with the change makers who are fighting for a racially just and equitable world.'

Let's see, founded by Paul Strasburg as IDEX (International Development Exchange) and then later changed name to Thousand Currents. And Paul says, 'the entire context of the work I had chosen to do was ever-expanding. I began to understand more deeply the role played by colonial history, concentration of economic power, and the decisions of government and institutions in the suffering of poor communities at home and around the world. I couldn't ignore what I had learned.'

Jet looked off in space, shook his head and said to himself, 'Just another bleeding heart liberal that hates colonial history and wants to concentrate economic power in HIS hands, because, of course, he is more compassionate, more caring than any other human on the planet and he only wants 50 million from me to help the poor. I bet the poor have not seen one percent of what he has collected in his lifetime and I further bet that his net worth would surpass even some of America's top politicians, like Nancy, Chuck and Joe.'

Jet thought, 'Well I now have a feel for Thousand Currents. See what Comrade Feng comes up with an hour from now.'

Feng's report was over fifty pages long and did not shed much more light on Thousand Currents and Paul Strasburg than Jet had been able to find. However, details on Thousand Currents' new finance director, one Susan Rosenburg, was quite interesting.

Reading Feng's report, Jet learned that Susan Lisa Rosenburg was born in 1955 to a middle-class Jewish family in Manhattan. Father was a dentist and mother a theatrical producer. She attended Walden, a progressive institution, and Barnard College. Later she became a drug counselor, eventually becoming licensed in the practice of Chinese medicine and acupuncture. At one point she worked in Harlem for the Black Acupuncture Advisory of North America. From late 1970 through mid 1980, she was active in the far-left revolutionary terrorist, May 19th Communist Organization which, according to the FBI, openly advocated the overthrow of the US government. She engaged in bombings of buildings and provided support to the Black Liberation Army.

In 1984 she was arrested and sentenced to 58 years in prison on weapons and explosive charges. She was a prime suspect in 1981 Brinks robbery where two policemen and a guard were killed, but the FBI could not make the charges stick. After serving 16 years her sentence was commuted on January 20, 2001, by Bill Clinton on his final day in office.

Feng's report went into mind-numbing detail on Rosenburg's work over the last 18 years, none of which changed Jet's initial assessment of Ms. Rosenburg. She was just another guilt-ridden white woman that wanted to spend her life righting the wrongs done to the blacks and by the way making sure that she was fully compensated along the way. It really was stupidity personified as her quest to be the black man's savior resulting in white men dying; of course that's OK because white men, like Washington and Jefferson were slave owners and every white man therefore is guilty of racism. Jet shook his head again and wondered, 'when will they ever realize that the black man's life outside Africa is always better than what it would have been under tribal rule where the Kings sold off his flock for pieces of gold.'

'Time to answer Lin,' he concluded.

Secure E-mail to Lin Lee.

I will be in Honolulu at the Royal Hawaiian Hotel on January 25/26. Look forward to seeing you.

CHAPTER
34 (Part B)

Jet thought to himself, as he sat in the beach-side bar, surrounded by the lush tropical grounds of the Royal Hawaiian Hotel in Waikiki, 'It's funny how some things never change.' He was remembering sitting at this very table with his wife, twenty-five years ago and everything was exactly the same. Palm tree filtered light, even at the sun's zenith, Mai Tai with a little Japanese umbrella garnish, probably the same Hawaiian waiter, just twenty-five years older, with a light breeze blowing off the blue, blue pacific. Breakers rolling up on the white sand with all manner of brown bodies in, on top and under the water. It was indeed paradise and he might just extend his stay as a week in Waikiki would not be bad.

He was interrupted by a familiar voice, "May I join you Comrade?" And there, stood Lin Lee in shorts and a garish Aloha shirt that only a tourist would buy. Jet grimaced but overcoming his initial reaction he smilingly replied, "I have been looking forward to seeing you. Come sit down and help me enjoy one of my favorite places in all this world."

Lin sat down and immediately was asked what he would like to drink and pointing at Jet's drink said. "I'll have one of those."

Jet opened, not with, how was the trip?, how are you doing? how goes the battle, but with, "So they want 50 million to allow us to help them?"

Taken back, Lin stammered and then looking around, wondering if the couple at the next table were CIA agents, he replied by merely nodding in the affirmative.

Jet continued, as if they were in a soundproof secure setting, "Are you familiar with the old American saying, 'never look a gift horse in the mouth'?"

Lin's look was blank and Jet continued, "You can tell the health and age of a horse by looking at its teeth. A gift horse can therefore, be a prize animal or ready for the glue factory. The person receiving the gift should not look in its mouth as it mig ht embarrass the giver."

Lin's comprehension level seemed to kick in as Jet continued, "Here we offer them money, personnel and a up and running organization and their reply is to stick out their hand and demand we pay for the privilege of working under their banner. If I told the President about this I know that his reaction would be negative but after thinking about it for a few days I am inclined to think we might string them along. After all, getting rid of Mr. T. is the goal, but on the other hand we know without our money or help they will still be doing everything in their power to accomplish the same goal. You are closer to the action, what's your take?"

"Well, Sir, I think it is pure and simple blackmail and we should distance ourselves as far from them as possible. After all, if we pay then they could blackmail us further by threatening to expose our involvement to the world, which in some circles would be a plus but which in most circles would be a negative. After all, we know how to organize street rallies, we know how to work the press and since we are oppressed Chinese students, just trying to better ourselves it is my opinion that 50 million could go a lot farther toward achieving our goal than giving it to BLM where fifty percent or more could go directly into Swiss bank accounts."

"Well said," Jet replied. Continuing he suggested, "Let's sleep on it and we will make a decision in the morning. Tonight, we are going to the Chinese Embassy as guests of the Ambassador and his wife. They have a cook I have been trying to hire for decades and believe me it will be a meal to be remember as Hawaiian and Chinese cuisine mixed is the absolute ultimate. Their limousine will pick us up at five and Lin, a little less casual dress would be appropriate."

Jet's description had not prepared Lin for Kailua pork, right out of the imu, (in ground cooker) or Huli-huli chicken, coconut pie or any one of the dozen of other dishes that the visitors were implored to try.

As they reluctantly pulled themselves from the comfort of the limo and stepped into the sweet night breezes under the Royal's grand porte-cochere Lin was kicking himself for not bringing his girlfriend, but putting that aside said to his employer, "Thank you for the experience of a lifetime. I shall never forget our dinner in Honolulu."

"Goodnight Lin. Breakfast at 0800 in the Terrace Restaurant, Just walk toward the beach and you will find it. Aloha."

34 (Part C)

Lin had sworn that he would never eat again after the Embassy stuffing but the breakfast buffet at the Royal was nothing to pass up and Jet was amazed at the amount of food that skinny body could consume.

Breakfast over, found the pair at the beach-side bar watching Waikiki beach come alive and the staggering array of brown and white bodies was a pleasure to behold. There were those, of course, who under penalty of law, should never be allowed out of their mumus but for the most part watching the beach come alive with tourists, from all over the world was a pleasing experience.

"Sir," purposely avoiding the comrade word, Lin replied, "I just think there are too many negatives and we should just let the association die a natural death. In other words, we just let our members work our plan of supporting any group that wants to see the current administration removed. If, in the process, we march with BLM supporters, so be it. The money we have available will see us through the next few months, as we are gearing up to make big pushes as soon as the impeachment process comes to center stage."

"So be it." was Jet's terse reply. "When will you be heading home?"

"I have a flight out tonight that will get me back home late tomorrow."

"How about you?"

Lin, of course did not need to know the travel schedule of Mr. China, but the damage was done, he had opened his big mouth so instead of apologizing for asking a stupid question he just smiled and waited.

Jet looked at his charge, knew what was going through his head, and replied. "The ambassador and I are taking a fishing boat to Molokai. It is always fun to chase a marlin or a big tuna or even an ono."

"I don't know the word ono, but recall hearing it last night."

"Well Lin, ono is the Hawaiian word for good but there is also a ono fish that is kin to barracuda, lots of sharp teeth, nasty fighter and when it's time to eat one, it is truly ono. Have a good trip and be in touch."

"Yes, Sir, you can count on it and thank you again for last night and for the opportunity to meet you here."

CHAPTER
35

During the first half of 2018, Jet spent over eighty percent of his time following the events in America and particularly the forever drama that seemed to hound Donald Trump on an almost hourly basis.

By June, when his nemesis was meeting in yet another summit with Kim Yang Choi and making world headlines, Jet was almost exhausted just trying to keep up with the heavy schedule that the man carried. Jet acknowledged, begrudging that you had to give him credit, he was a worker and as the international scene developed and the domestic side heated up, he never seemed to lose his focus.

The Democrats threw up thousands of blockades that would cause the normal human to stumble, but Trump just kept knocking down the hurdles and flashing toward the finish line.

In late June, a summit with Vladimir Putin was a foot-dance affair that was put on tender hooks when three days before the summit Rod Rosenstein, the Deputy Attorney General, announced indictments of twelve Russian officers for their efforts in the 2016 Democratic National Committee e-mail leaks scandal. Then two days before the meeting a group of top Senate Democrats urged Trump not to meet with Putin one-on-one and during an interview on the eve of the summit Trump was asked who America's biggest foe is. He said Russia is a foe in certain aspects, the European union is the biggest trade foe and then on the morning of the summit Trump tweeted, 'Russia, USA relationships have never been worse', and blamed it on the witch hunt currently going forward under the Special Counsel investigation.

Jet was perplexed that Trump cited the European Union as America's biggest trade foe, when he seldom missed a chance to knock China and their unfair trade practices. 'Could the line be softening?' was just one of the thoughts that raced around Mr. China's head as he tried to put it all in perspective so he could better understand the enemy.

By October the trade agreement with Canada and Mexico was big news for the world but for China it was the tariff increases made in June and July that were currently wreaking havoc on the Christmas rush. Over the Clinton and Obama years, Christmas had turned into one of Chinas biggest economic booms, in that nine out of ten Christmas decorations purchased in America, were made in China. The tariffs of 25% on 50 billion, followed by 25% on an additional 34 billion and before year end 16 billion more meant that in just six months a staggering burden had been piled onto 100 million dollars of China's exports.

Jet had been hearing the woes of the big Christmas suppliers and in tight margin items, such as Christmas decorations, the tariffs meant the slim profit margins were now bleeding red. The government in Beijing had to actually pass out subsidies to keep some of the manufacturers from going out of business.

Jet thought, 'Yanlin was right, we cannot survive eight years of this. Four is going to be hard enough. What's going on with impeachment?' After all Jet had spoken directly with Adam Schiff, earlier in the year, and was promised that the impeachment ship would sail, it was just a matter of time and money. Jet had directed millions into the Democratic coffers and all he had to show for it was shifty palms always reaching out for more.

By December, Trump was able to announce that the ISIS was defeated and he signaled his intention to withdraw all 2,000 U.S. troops that had been supporting the SDF in Syria. By March the final holdout, Baghouz fell, formally ending the Caliphate's claim to any territory.

Jet, in a conversation with President Hu, just before their Group of five first meeting in February of 2019, had made the point that with all the heel nipping and all the probes and investigations Trump was still able to stay focused and defeat ISIS. A defeat that Obama maintained was going to take years and years to accomplish.

The February 2019, Group of Five meeting was held once again at the bunker complex and happened to coincide with the latest summit between Trump and North Korea's portly leader in Hanoi, Vietnam. President Hu had a private talk, a few days before the summit, with Kim but was unable to come up with any clear understanding as to where the talks might go or what Kim was thinking. It was frustrating for the Chinese President but Kim was being closed mouth about his long-term strategy and President Hu did not feel the time was right to dictate terms to Kim as he was being more belligerent than usual. Push-come-to-shove, President Hu knew he could play the oil, food or electricity cards and get the boys' attention, but that would come later.

In the final analysis, it boiled down to Washington's unwillingness to take the first step on sanctions relief. There was also the fact that in the current political environment there was a risk that momentum for an agreement would be lost in a sea of competing interests. The foremost of which was the administration's concerns over impeachment.

With the big events of the day running their own course President Hu, addressing the Group of Five asked, "anyone have any insight as to when the impeachment hammer might fall on Mr. Trump?"

Jet, knew a cue when he heard it, and replied, "Comrades the wheels of progress turn slowly but if I were a betting man I would put my money on the Democrats. From what I hear the process will be well underway by mid-January and be over before this time next year,"

Lin Wong asked, "Comrade, if that is the case, what do you expect the final outcome to look like?"

"Acquittal, the Senate is controlled by the Republicans and while some of them are Trump haters they risk too much to vote against him but it will be such a big negative for the President; one that I don't see him able to overcome, and he will lose come November of 2020. The Tiger option is still a distinct possibility and the decision that has to come soon. I think I can speak for the President when I say it may just be our last line of defense, because Comrades I can be wrong."

Everyone looked at President Hu. Would he confirm Jet's assessment or would he hedge?

President Hu knew the ball was in his court and this was just as good a time as any to make a final decision. Standing he said, "Comrades, in early December 2019 we will release the Tiger. I know that many of our countrymen may pay the ultimate price, but I consider this assault kin to a shooting war and we all know that war equals death and casualties."

A pin dropping would have been like a clap of thunder. Dead silence hung on the words the President had just uttered. Each individual knew that they were witness to a Declaration of War and each man was conscious of his own labored breathing.

"The people selected me to lead and to preside over this great land and I will not let them down. Jet, will you close out this meeting?"

Not waiting for a reply, the President exited the conference room, removed his coat on his way through his office, and walked out into his manufactured illusion and hopeful escape. As he stood on the edge of the pool, letting the waterfall sounds drench him he wondered out loud, 'Will time remove every obstacle and judge me fairly?' Not one ancestor chose to reply.

CHAPTER
36

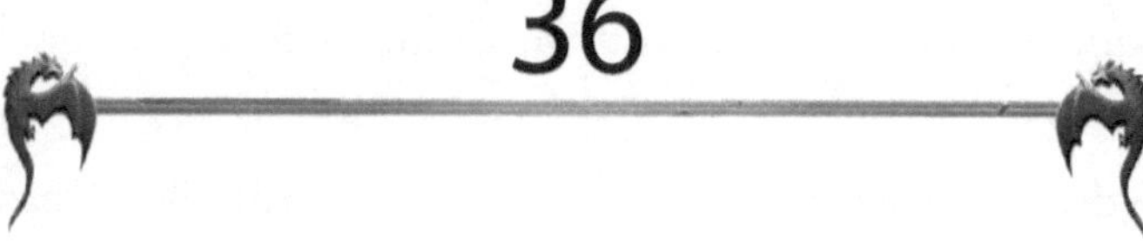

Jet, of course was not surprised when the news of the day was that Trump had not only dodged the Mueller bullets, but the whole damn clip. Thirty of the smartest lawyers in Washington, all who hated his guts, were not even able to pin a speeding citation on Wile E. Coyote. It was downright disgusting when you consider how much the Sterling report cost and how much Ambassador Xu Qiliang had spent greasing the skids. What a waste. Then out loud he broke the silence in his office and shouted, "What a utter waste." Raised eyebrows in his reception area seldom heard outbursts from Mr. Cool so Jet's entire staff was on high alert and everyone wanted to know what had caused this unusual behavior.

Jet hit the intercom button and barked, "What time is it in Washington?"

An immediate reply from a soothing female voice said, "Two a.m. Sir."

"Get Ambassador Xu Qiliang on the line now."

"Yes, Sir."

A sleep filled voice finally came over the speaker asking, "What may I do for you Comrade?"

"You can tell me how he did it? How in the hell did he dodge all of our bullets, how?"

Sputtering and knowing his life could be on the line, Ambassador Xu replied, in the most business like voice he could command on such short notice by saying, "I can only assume he was not guilty."

Jet did not like the answer and black hot bullets pierced the phone. He visualized the Ambassador and his sexy wife being machine-gunned down by a firing squad and red blood spilling down a set of steps and turning a river red. Biting his lip he said, "I want a full report of all the money you and Lin Lee have spent on this goose-less chase and I want it before I go home in three hours."

The receiver clicked dead and the ambassador had visions of he and his sexy wife being mowed down by a firing squad.

Within minutes the embassy came alive, with shouting and screams and across town Lin Lee was hastily dressing, ordering a taxi and saying his could-be-final goodbyes to his wife and child.

An hour into the deadline Lin Lee and Ambassador Xu were in the secure conference room trying to find a number that was somewhat accurate. The Ambassador had spent hundreds of thousands if not millions on Ohr, Comey, Strozk, Page, McCabe, Simpson, Brennan, Clapper and all of their Department Heads and subheads, assistants and a whole host of their entourage that like to feel important.

The accounting system was extremely loose, which had allowed the Ambassador, over the years, to send healthy chunks of money to his Swiss bank account on an annual basis. Most of the activity, i.e. the expenses had to be from memory rather than hard documents.

Two hours into the deadline the two men were sweating profusely and on the ragged edge of irritation and the Ambassador excoriated Jet's entire ancestral lineage and then, red-faced, explained that he did not mean that, rather he was just frustrated.

Lin Lee announced, almost apologetically, "Comrade my figure is 145 million."

The Ambassador looked beat, what could he do, he would just have to go with his best guess and then get the staff to find backup that would support his guess. It occurred to the Ambassador that he might appear in a better light if his figure was less. Consulting a pile of yellow tablets, shuffling documents here and there the Ambassador looked at Lin Lee and said, "My figure is 93 million."

Picking up the house phone he ordered, "Call Jet How Chung." The voice in the outer office confirmed the request and shortly on the speaker phone the Ambassador heard, "Yes!"

Comrade, Lin and I have been reviewing the documentation and Lin says his total expenses come to 145 and Comrade my expenses are 93 million for a total of 238."

"Thank you; I can add."

The silence seemed endless. Finally, Jet announced in a calm and steady voice, "Please e-mail the details. I shall expect to see your reports on my desk in the morning. Goodnight Comrades." Click, the line went dead and the two men stared across the table each wondering if he was looking at a dead man. Both were flogging the self-abnegation buttons; neither had a clue what to do first and then Lin blurted out, "We only have until 7pm, that's just fourteen hours. I don't think I can make it, but I can't make it happen sitting here so I am gone Comrade." With that said he scooped up his notes and raced for the exit.

In Beijing, Jet put on his coat, said goodnight to the staff and walked toward his limousine with a curious smile and thinking to himself, "I wonder if they will turn gray by morning or if they will even be alive?"

<h1 style="text-align:center">CHAPTER
37</h1>

The CNN skirted anchor was almost breathless and tears were not far from welling up in her eyes but she charged full steam ahead on the subject of terrible Trump and how he had used Ukraine in an effort to smear that saint among saints, Joseph Biden. It was the headline around the world and Jet and Yanlin, watching from Yanlin's office in the bunker complex, were chuckling among themselves.

Yanlin, the People's President remarked, "If I had thirty national and international news organizations nipping at my heels, 24/7, I don't think I would last a week. How in the hell does he do it Jet?"

Jet shaking his head replied, "If I knew I would bottle it and become a millionaire overnight. It is truly amazing and mark my words comrade it will be ancient history in just weeks because there will be even a bigger fish to fry, like impeachment. I spoke with Adam Schiff last week and he assured me that by early January the House will vote and the Senate will have to consider the charges."

"Will any of it stick, comrade?"

Jet looked at his leader, gave him a big smile and said, "No. He will walk away no worse for wear other than the polls, right up to election eve will show him losing and losing badly to Sleepy Joe as Trump calls him. I do not, however, believe that the pundits are right. In the West people vote their pocketbooks and that is an area where he has excelled. By reducing regulations, slapping tariffs on us, getting companies to abandoned their foreign factories, he has crafted an economy that makes the Obama years look like dirty rice." Pausing and looking directly at his leader Jet continued, "And that, Yanlin is why our tiger Zhanlue is so terribly important. I have everything in place and await only your final word."

Yanlin Hu, President and Supreme leader of The People's Republic of China looked at his long time friend and associate and said. "I have been thinking that since Christmas is such an important date for the worlds' Christians we should honor their celebration by releasing our tiger on Christmas Day." Smiling the President asked, "Will you take care of the operational details and final notifications?"

"Of course Comrade."

CENTER FOR DISEASE CONTROL AND PREVENTION

Volume 26, Number 6

EPIDEMIOLOGY OF CORONAVIRUS DISEASE IN GANSU PROVINCE, CHINA

The outbreak of coronavirus disease (COVID-19) was first reported on December 31, 2019, in Wuhan, China. Within a few weeks the virus had spread rapidly throughout China and within one month to several other countries, including Italy, the United States and Germany. Difficulty controlling such aggressive spread resulted partly from the size of Wuhan, which has a full-time population of 9 million and a transient population of an additional 5.1 million, for a total population of 14 million. Wuhan is located in central China and has a wide range of transportation links, including airplanes, trains, interstate buses, and private transportation. In an attempt to reduce virus transmission, on January 23, 2020, authorities locked down Wuhan, but by that time 5 million persons had already left. Reasons for leaving included returning to hometowns for the Chinese New Year or leaving for holidays.

(above direct quote from Center For Disease Control web site.)

Part of the 5 million people that left Wuhan, between December 25 and January 23, 2020, were over one hundred thousand government workers who had received overseas travel vouchers, as a year-end bonus program. Many of the government workers used their bonuses to fly from Wuhan Tianhe International airport to Italy and other points in Europe, but thousands also chose America as their destination of choice. The bonus program had been sponsored and funded by the central government through the offices of the President's Chief Advisor, one Jet How Chung.

Dr. John Brownstein, an epidemiologist at Boston's Children's Hospital said on ABC News.

"This data shows that 3,200 flights flew from China to the U.S., including more than 1,000 flights that went to Los Angeles and nearly 500 each landed in San Francisco and New York - all three were among the eventual hot spots of the COVID-19 outbreak in the U.S.. More than 100 flights from China arrived in six other American cities: Chicago, Seattle, Detroit, Dallas, Washington D.C. and Newark, N.J."

According to travel data obtained by ABC News, those flights translated to more than 761,000 Chinese nationals entering the U.S. and Americans returning home from the People's Republic of China during that critical four-month period.

(Above written by John Kelly and Pierre Thomas for ABC News)

Jet spent most of Christmas day at the Chaoxue lab with Director Yang overseeing the schedule for container releases and with the chief technician that controlled the satellites. The technicians explained to Jet that in 24 hours a satellite will cross over the same two spots on the equator every day and thus it would only take a few weeks for all 4 million containers, that had been scattered across the world, to receive their release signals. The tech's were quick to point out that only those containers, in warehouses or at truck stops or waiting to be unloaded would be effective virus spreaders. Out of the over four million units, at least 20 to 25 percent would be effective and Jet and his staff accepted that as a reasonable result for the small investment made.

In the month before the Trump administration banned most non-U.S. citizens from entering the United States from China, American and Chinese carriers operated roughly 325 weekly flights between the two countries. By mid-February the number of flights had dropped to only about 20 weekly scheduled flights, all flown by Chinese airlines.

Before departing the Chaoxue complex, Jet e-mailed his leader a short message that read. 'Tiger escaped his lair.'

CHAPTER
38

The articles of impeachment against Donald Trump passed the House of Representatives by a margin of 230 to 197 on December 18, 2019. On February 5, 2020, the Senate voted for acquittal and that ended the three and one-half year witch hunt.

It had all began on January 2017, when a Democratic representative from Texas, one Al Green, announced an impeachment inquiry. His call resonated with Democrats around the country and for three and a half years they whipped the pony but in the end their horse never made the finish line.

Jet had told President Hu that it would never fly but both men heaped hope on hope. In the final analysis Teflon Trump skated out of the arena flashing victory signs. That coupled with all his other bullet dodging efforts convinced the People's Republic leader that his only recourse was to use his secret weapon.

When the virus emerged from the Wuhan area the World Heath Organization down played its potential and when Donald Trump stopped flights from China, Nancy Pelosi, Joe Biden and the fake news organization accused him of being a racist and Nancy even went to China town, in San Francisco, and walked around hugging Chinese visitors to prove what a racist America had for a President.

The spring and summer of 2020, saw the virus flash around the world and every day the count of the infected and the death toll rises and almost no one thinks that preface mask life will ever return to America. Unemployment is up, schools are closed, thousands of businesses will never reopen, and America is hurting like it has never hurt. Couple that with the Black Lives Matter movement, the invasions of major American cities by bands of protesters whose weapon of choice is fire coupled with smash and grab. One protester even admitted that he gets a monthly check from George Soros for leading uprisings.

Americans watch as their heritage is being trashed by the mush-filled minds that even pull down statutes of civil rights leaders in their quest to out-riot their buddies in Portland, Seattle or New York.

Defund the police is the current cry which really means "Lets not have a judicial system" as it may be unfair as well. How do you run a judicial system without the police is a question that no one asks. So if you are charged with a crime and you have your day in court, you can just show up and make your case. No police to make the process orderly, no police to protect the judge or the jury in cases where they make a ruling against you and you decide to beat them up or kill them, who's to stop you?

It is call ANARCHY i.e. a state of disorder due to absence or nonrecognition of authority.

The Supreme Court will not be able to function, as without police their chambers can be broken into and they too can be at the mercy of the mob. Wonder what the liberals on the court will think of that turn of events?

If you are a House or Senate member you best not set foot in Washington as there will be mobs of mindless trolls that can topple you with a rope as they have done to Grant, Jefferson, Columbus and even Mary and Jesus.

Jet and President Hu spent long evenings discussing the above and time and time again congratulated themselves on the past decisions to remove guns from their Chinese citizens. Jet, pondering all the questions and remarked, "We can survive mob riots, like those going on in Hong Kong because they have no guns. In America there are 120 guns for every 100 people which comes up to about 393 million guns. If each gun would kill just one soldier you need a very big army to quell an uprising. We will win in Hong Kong because we have the guns and because we don't care how many die in the process."

Looking deeply with flashing eyes Jet closed his thesis by saying, "Yanlin, I have a confession."

The President of the People's Republic of China looked at his old war horse and with unusual compassion asked, "Are you going to share it with me or keep me in the dark?"

Jet with almost tears, in the corner of each black darting eye, looked down at the floor, then stood up and announced, "I am resigning my posts and will be moving myself and my family to a remote village in Tibet as I have failed you; I have failed the people you lead and I have failed myself and you need no daily reminders of my failures."

President Hu stood, came face-to-face with his faithful friend and was about to reply, when Jet continued, "Yanlin, I would walk through hell for you and our cause, but I can no longer continue for I know, I know as certain as I know that I stand here in your presence, that I have been wrong and that all my efforts and the millions of dollars we spent were not enough and therefore I must retreat where I can lick my wounds and die."

"Now Jet, what could be so important to bring you to this life changing point?"

Jet smiled at his friend and leader, not his usual diabolical smile of victory but a smile blended over remorse and said in a soft low voice, "Donald Trump will win reelection and will set back our hundred-year Zhanlu by decades. I let you and the country down and I shall go to my grave knowing that I failed."

Jet was, for once in his life, wrong. When the results of the American election were certified and Joseph Biden was set to become the 46th President of the United States of America, President Hu sent Jet How a letter, by personnel courier, with a check drawn on the Bank of China for 100 million dollars. The note attached read:

"For my loyal comrade who changed the world forever. I have no doubts that your actions will lead to our enemy being mortally wounded without us having to fire a shot. We will watch them go

back to energy dependency, under their green banner, which will lead to massive inflation and supply chain nightmares. They will abandon their twenty-year commitments in Afghanistan, they will have nothing to say when Putin invades Ukrainian and Europe will freeze during the 2022 winter after the Nord Stream pipeline is fractured."

"Biden and the Penn-Biden Center will be our greatest asset in our quest to rule the planet, starting with our takeover of Taiwan before his term expires."

"You truly are a national treasure and a genius."

Yanlin